The Twisted Ones

LAWRENCE BLOCK
writing as Andrew Shaw

THE TWISTED ONES

LAWRENCE BLOCK writing as ANDREW SHAW

Copyright © 1961 Lawrence Block

All Rights Reserved.

Cover and Interior Design by QA Productions

A LAWRENCE BLOCK PRODUCTION

Classic Erotica

21 Gay Street
Candy
Gigolo Johnny Wells
April North
Carla
A Strange Kind of Love
Campus Tramp
Community of Women
Born to be Bad
College for Sinners
Of Shame and Joy
A Woman Must Love
The Adulterers
Kept
The Twisted Ones
High School Sex Club
I Sell Love
69 Barrow Street
Four Lives at the Crossroads
Circle of Sinners
A Girl Called Honey
Sin Hellcat
So Willing

CLASSIC EROTICA #15

THE TWISTED ONES

Lawrence Block

CHAPTER 1

Grantland was tired. He slumped in the easy chair in the living room, his eyes half closed, his heavy body relaxed in something close to sleep. In front of him images gamboled on the screen of the 21-inch television set. The program was a western. The lead character, appropriately long and lanky, had been "just passin' through" when trouble had beckoned its bony finger. Now he was neck-deep in a mess of outlaws, women, and crooked sheriffs. It was too much for Grantland to follow, and he had given up long ago.

Dave Grantland was 34. For ten of those thirty-four years he had been married to a very beautiful woman with long silver-blonde hair and an extremely voluptuous figure. She was in the kitchen right now and he could see her very vividly in his mind as she finished sterilizing the area after the experience of dinner. She would be bending over the sink, her breasts straining against the front of her sheer blouse, her buttocks tight and plump in her shorts. She was a girl who tended toward extremes—very large breasts, very slender waist, very full hips, very long legs, very blonde hair, very blue eyes. Her appearance was so incredibly sensual, so much the personification of a Hollywood stereotype of sexual perfection, that it was hard for a man to look at her without getting a little embarrassed. If a girl could be said to look too sexy, Nancy Grantland was the girl.

His eyes closed, rejecting the western. His mind studied Nancy's figure and mentally removed the blouse and the shorts. The clever fingers of his brain then took off the shoes and socks, the thin panties, the unnecessary bra. The effect of all this was very interesting. Now, in his mind, he saw her—still at the sink, still washing the dishes, but now quite naked. She reached for a spoon at the bottom of the sink and her breasts bumped into cold porcelain. She dried a dish with a dish towel and the end of the towel brushed her body, trailed between her swollen thighs, touching her.

A strange picture.

Grantland's reaction was every bit as strange. He thought of his wife, thought of her body, thought of the marvelous ways in which she made love. He thought of this and he thought of that, giving full rein to both memory and imagination.

And he hoped, desperately, that Nancy would not want to make love that night.

The Gavilans were out for the evening.

Fred and Joanne Gavilan lived at 134 Aberdeen Drive, which is a quiet tree-shaded street in Mataquois, which is a middle-class suburb of New York located on Long Island. Since the Grantlands lived at 138 Aberdeen Drive, the two couples were next door neighbors. They were also fairly close friends. Not too close, because the Gavilans were slightly different from the Grantlands.

Fred Gavilan made a little less money than Dave Grantland, was three years younger, and had a two-year-old infant.

Because of the infant, a monotonous little boy named Craig, the Gavilans had hired a baby-sitter. This particular baby-sitter was sixteen years old. Her name was Lucy King. It was her job, simple enough, to remain at 134 Aberdeen Drive with Craig until Fred and Joanne Gavilan returned home from the movie they had gone to watch. Since Craig spent twenty out of every twenty-four hours in an unconscious state, this was far from the most difficult job in the world.

To help Lucy avoid losing her mind, the Gavilans encouraged her to do certain things while "sitting" for Craig. She was permitted to watch the television set, read any of the books in the Gavilan bookcase, do her homework, or play records. While the Gavilans might also have permitted Lucy to have company while she sat, Lucy was wise beyond her sixteen years.

She did not bother to ask them.

She had company now. The company was a boy named Joe Turley. He was one year older than Lucy and one year ahead of her in school. He was also a boy with plans. His far-ranging plans included going away to college, learning to be a dentist, and making as much money as he possibly could. He also had short-range plans. His most elaborate short-range plan, at the moment, was the seduction of Lucy King.

They were sitting on the couch. The television set was on, and they were watching the same western that Dave Grantland was blatantly ignoring in the house next door. They, too, were paying little attention to the western. They were sitting close together, and Joe's arm was around Lucy, and Lucy was wondering just how far she was going to let him get.

It was a problem. She *liked* Joe, liked him very much, but he was not the only boy she liked any more than he was the only boy she necked with. Whether she liked him or not wasn't really too consequential right now, she knew. What mattered was how far she was going to let him get with her. It was a tricky problem. She knew full well that he would go as far as he possibly could, with the eventual aim of getting her panties off. But she didn't think she wanted that to happen. It would hurt, for one thing, and it might get her pregnant, for another, and, for a third, it would thoroughly demolish her reputation as a Nice Girl.

But, she realized, it would probably feel wonderful.

"You watching that?"

"Huh?"

"The television," he said. "You watching it or should I turn it off?"

"Oh," she said. "You can turn it off. You want to play records or something?"

He got up, walked to the television set and flicked a knob. The sound stopped at once. Then the picture got smaller and smaller until only a tiny dot remained in the center of the screen. The dot stayed there for a long time.

Joe returned to the couch.

For a moment things were very awkward. But only for a moment. Then he reached for her and, hungrily, she came to him. His mouth was warm on hers and his arm curled around her, clutching her close to him.

They kissed.

Lucy was not entirely innocent in the ways of the world and the hungers of the flesh. She had been kissed before, and she had been French-kissed before, and she had found the experience pleasant enough.

But this time it was different. There was a sureness, a directness in the embrace of Joe Turley that shook her up more than a little. Deftly, professionally, his tongue slipped between her soft lips and forced them apart. She had decided to keep her teeth closed—at least for a little while, just to show him she wasn't too easy—but before she knew it her mouth was wide open and his hot tongue was probing deeply into her mouth, tasting the girlish sweetness of her.

He knew damn well what he was doing. His tongue probed here, touched there, and everywhere it touched her it set her on fire. A warm glow went over her entire body and her breathing became deeper. Her pulse rate went up and her skin was flushed.

God, she thought. One kiss and he had her ready to climb the walls. What was the matter with her?

He released her as suddenly as he had grabbed her and they sat staring at each other. His eyes were bold, studying her firm young breasts. "Nice," he murmured softly. "You got a nice pair, Lucy. Real nice."

She shivered. His words were coarse, vulgar, but they were reaching her nevertheless. "Stop it," she said.

"Why?"

"I don't like that kind of talk."

"The hell you don't."

"I—"

"You like the talk," he said, "and you like to do more than talk. I know about you."

"What do you know?"

"That you like it," he said mysteriously.

She took a deep breath and released it slowly. She put a hand on her hair, as if to reassure herself that it was neatly combed, and stared at him. He looked at her hair. It was black, cut short in an Italian style, and it looked good on her. Then he looked again at her breasts. She was wearing a scarlet sweater and when he stared at it she felt as though her face was turning the color of the sweater.

"Why don't you take off that sweater?" he suggested. "I'm just going to have to take it off for you."

"Don't talk like that!"

He didn't seem to notice. "That's the start," he said. "Then I'll take off your bra and give you a good feeling. Then your skirt. Then your pants. And then I'll push you back on the couch and show you what it's all about."

"Joe—"

"Come here," he said.

She didn't want to. She was afraid, but at the same time her body burned with eagerness to taste the caresses he was prepared to give her. She was afraid, but fear alone could not override her desire.

She went to him.

They kissed again. This time her mouth was open at once and her lips welcomed his tongue. This time her arms wound around him and held him close. She felt his strong young body pressing against her breasts. The tips of them thrilled with the contact.

He released her. Then his hand reached for her, his fingers curling around the full sweetness of one breast. She pushed his hand away once and he grinned.

When he reached for her again she did not push him away. His fingers stroked, tensing and relaxing, and she let herself get caught up in a swirling of madcap desires. He touched, stroked, and her heart sang.

Nancy Grantland hung up the dish towel on the hook, took off her soiled apron and dropped it down the laundry chute. She stopped for a moment in the bathroom and studied herself in the mirror. She ran a comb through her hair, splashed a few drops of water on her face.

She was very pretty and she knew it.

Very pretty. So pretty that she was accustomed to the stares of men who passed her on the street. They were something that she had grown used to over the years, one of the normal parts of the life of an extraordinarily beautiful woman. She walked through life wearing the eyes of other men on her breasts and belly and thighs. It was part of the game.

Now, standing in front of the mirror, she played a game with herself. It was not a new game by any means but one she played often, several times a week at the very least. She looked into the mirror and the mirror looked back. She talked silently to the mirror image, forming words with her full red lips making no audible sound.

You are a woman, she said. *A beautiful woman. You look like a woman and you talk like a woman and you move like a woman and you act like a woman.*

She sighed. Then she began again. *No one could think otherwise. Nobody could possibly suspect anything else. And there's no reason why they should. That all happened a long time ago. It's over and done with. It doesn't mean anything any more.*

But was that the truth? If it meant nothing, as she told herself it did, why did she have to make the point again and again, over and over, mumbling soundless words at a mirror in a persistent attempt at auto-hypnosis?

Perhaps the lady doth protest too much. Perhaps the lady is not a lady at all. Perhaps the leopard cannot change its spots, and perhaps—

Trembling, she turned from the mirror. It was nothing, nothing at all. She was behaving like a child. And Dave would prove it to her. Dave, who knew nothing about it, would prove to her how silly it was for her to worry. Dave would take care of her, and Dave would be good to her, and in Dave's arms everything would be all right again.

She sighed again. Dave had been so cold to her lately, so distant, so remote. She tried to tell herself that it meant nothing, that Dave had business worries on his mind, that the advertising business was a hectic business and that Dave, holding down a hot spot at his agency, was having more than his share of headaches lately. It wasn't that he didn't want her, didn't need her as much as ever. It was just that he was being dragged under by too many worries and too many problems. He still wanted her. He still needed her. And he would take care of her.

She left the bathroom and walked into the living room. He

was sitting on a chair in front of the television set. She crossed over in front of him and sat down on the couch, curling her long legs under her and smiling at him.

"Good program?"

He looked up, as if noticing her presence for the first time, and shook his head. "Terrible," he said. "I'd turn it off except one of our accounts is sponsoring. I want to see how the commercials look."

"If the show is so bad, why sponsor it?"

"The ratings," he said. "According to the ratings, more morons watch this show than any other in the same time slot. The ratings are a sort of God Thing for atheists. Ginchy Hair Crème sponsors this hour of trivia so that all the morons will put Ginchy on their heads."

"Does it work?"

"Which? The program works. I guess. Ginchy's reported sky-rocketing sales. Ginchy's happy, we're happy, and all is well. Incidentally, we won a round on Ginchy. It's made by Kallett Brothers, Inc. I picked up a hundred shares of Kallett at 31½ the day we landed the account. It hit forty yesterday."

"That's good," she said, not quite sure what he was talking about. Whenever he talked about stocks she was lost. She merely took it for granted that he knew what he was doing with their money. He always gave her whatever money she needed to run the house, paid her a weekly allowance of private money for herself, and seemed to have enough left over so that money was never a prime worry. Still, it bothered her from time to time that she didn't know anything about their financial situation. It seemed as though she ought to, as though it was another area of their marriage in which she was not participating and which she ought to share with him.

"Damned good," he said. "If it keeps moving we just might get a new car this year."

"Really?"

He nodded.

"That would be nice. Another Pontiac?"

"I was thinking about an Olds."

"Honestly?"

"Why not? We're making money. What can you spend money on besides status symbols? A 29-inch television set, a big car, a fur coat—status symbols. Can't tell the paupers from the successes without a status symbol. Getcha status symbols here. Over here, folks. Motivation Research is right on the stick, folks, turning out just the status symbol for your personal psychological state. Get 'em while they're hot, folks."

She laughed uncertainly. "An Olds would be nice," she admitted. "The Hedgers have an Olds. They like it."

"That settles it," he said. "Then we'll get one." The sarcasm in his voice was a shade too light for her to detect it. She was tired of the subject anyway. An Olds *would* be nice, admittedly, but there was something that would be even nicer.

"Dave," she said.

He looked at her.

"Come sit by me," she said.

He stood up and walked over to her. He sat down next to her and she rubbed up against him like a kitten. "I missed you today," she said. "I missed you so much. The house was like a tomb. Nothing to do."

"Poor kid."

"Sometimes I wish I hadn't quit my job," she went on. "If we could have had kids it would have been different. Something to do at home. But this way I go nuts. I clean the house till I'm blue. And then I stare at the damn television set until my eyes water. It's boring."

She rarely mentioned her own inability to have children, not because it would hurt Dave but because it hurt her. It wasn't Dave's fault—he was fertile enough, but she herself was barren. Often she felt inadequate as a result. Inadequate, incomplete, only partially a woman.

"You couldn't go on working," he told her. "Going all the way into Manhattan for a job. Silly."

"Maybe I could find something here on the Island."

"Maybe," he said.

"It would be better than sitting around the house," she said. "It isn't just that I get bored. I feel so damned useless. It's rotten, feeling as though you're not accomplishing anything."

"That's silly."

"Is it?"

"Sure," he said. "Look, suppose you got a job clerking in a store, something like that. What the hell would you accomplish that way? What victory for humanity would you win as a sales clerk? What great works would you accomplish?"

"At least I'd bring in some extra money."

"Forty a week?"

"That's better than nothing," she said. "Isn't it?"

"Of course it is. But you shouldn't have to kill yourself for a lousy forty a week."

"You don't understand," she said.

"I don't?"

"I would be killing myself a lot less if I went to work every day. That's what I mean."

"Well, if that's what you want—"

"Maybe I'll look for something tomorrow," she said.

"Okay."

"I might even find something interesting. It isn't as though I have to take the first job that comes along."

"Sure," he said. "Take your time. Wait until you get what you want."

Her approach shifted. She turned toward him, leaned against him, looked up at him. She remembered the monologue she had delivered to the mirror and she shivered, not entirely unpleasantly. She smiled.

"I know what I want," she purred.

She watched his eyes roam over her, studying the breasts, the waist.

"What do you want?"

She ran a hand over his shirt front. His body was still young, strong. She told herself how much she liked his body, repeating the desire mentally to make it real.

"I want you to take me to bed," she said.

"Now?"

"Now."

"I'm a little tired, Nancy."

"I'll wake you up," she said. "I'll wake you up. Let's go upstairs, Dave. Now."

•　　　•　　　•

The scene had changed slightly in Fred and Joanne Gavilan's living room. Now, on the floor beside the couch, a sweater and a bra lay in a limp heap. On top of the couch a boy's body lay over a girl's body.

Lucy's head was swimming. She was bare to the waist now. It was as far as she had ever permitted a boy to go with her, and Joe Turley had gone that far with enviable persistence. He did not seem at all likely to stop there. She wondered dimly if he was going to stop at all. He was a very smooth and accomplished young man. His hands were skillful.

First he had kissed her intensely. Then he had manipulated her plump breasts through the red sweater. It had not taken him too long before his hands had snuck beneath the sweater, rubbing the smooth skin of her back and stomach, fastening on the breasts held in her bra.

Then the sweater had disappeared. It was just as well, of course. Otherwise the sweater might stretch, and she didn't want to ruin the sweater—it was a good one, fairly expensive and almost new. So she permitted him to draw it over her head, pulling the wool over her eyes, as it were.

The bra had followed shortly thereafter.

Then things had really grown exciting. His deft hands on her bare breasts were infinitely more pleasurable than they had been when first the sweater and then the bra had served as a barrier between his skin and hers.

It was better with nothing in the way. And he knew just what to do to make it as exciting as possible. He took her breasts in his hands and squeezed, then relaxed, then squeezed again. He took the nipple of one breast between thumb and forefinger and began to play with it, teasing her.

Then the other nipple. She reacted in the same manner, her nipple growing rigid with desire, and the more he stroked her and played with her the more her desire grew within her, spreading through her body almost magically, inflaming her and making her burn with pure animal heat.

She knew what she wanted to do next. No one had ever done it to her before, not really. Once a boy had given her a quick kiss upon her breast, but that had been only a teaser, a quick caress before she took control of the situation and made him stop. But it had been pleasant, and she hoped that Joe would do what the other boy had started to do.

He stroked her some more, his fingers clever with her. And then he did what she wanted him to do. His mouth crept from her mouth down over her throat and shoulder to her breast.

He kissed her and she shivered.

He began to kiss again, his mouth flitting from one breast to the other and back again. It was even better than she had imagined and she knew that it was dangerous, very dangerous. If he kept this up she was going to lose control. And if she lost control he was going to do it to her and there would be no way to stop him.

She half-hoped he would do it to her. She wondered what it was like and she wanted to find out. But at the same time she half-hoped she would be able to stop him. Her virginity, she knew, was not the sort of thing she could regain once she lost it. It was easy enough for a girl to lose her virginity and well nigh impossible to get it back again.

But—

"Nice," he was murmuring. "Nicest little boobs in the world. Real nice, Lucy."

Her passion dropped for a second. It would be much better, she thought, if he didn't talk. He was coarse and vulgar, and the words he used only made her feel cheap. But he stopped talking then and went back to kissing and caressing and her passion built up again within her. She decided that he was much better at kissing and caressing than he was at talking.

Then his hand was on her knee.

This, she knew at once, was the danger point. His hand was on her knee, and soon his hand would begin the momentous journey to the North, traveling cleverly beneath her skirt. His hand would be heading for the promised land, and if it got there, then there was no way at all of telling what might happen to her. So she ought to stop him right away.

But she didn't want to.

The hand felt nice on her knee. He was squeezing her knee rhythmically while he went on kissing her nipples and it was very enjoyable indeed.

When his hand crept midway up her thigh she still did not want to stop him.

It was better to relax. Better to let things happen, better to enjoy the feelings that coursed over her. The touch of his feverish fingers on the soft, smooth, silky skin of her thigh was delicious. The hand moved upward slowly, very slowly, and she loved the touch.

Closer—

"No," she said, suddenly, her determination surprising her. And, suiting actions to words, her legs closed tight, pinning the hand in place and preventing its progress to the promised land. Her own hands lifted his face from her breast and her whole body went tense, rigid.

"No," she said again.

And he made a mistake.

"Please," he said. "Please, Lucy. Honey, please let me touch you. I won't hurt you. I won't make you go all the way, honest, I won't, I just want to touch you. Just let me touch a little, Lucy. Please let me. You'll like it, you'll like how it feels, it'll make you feel good. I swear you'll like it. And I won't try to do anything you don't want me to do. I promise it, Lucy. I promise I won't!"

It was not what he should have said.

She remained there, very tense, and she knew that he had made a great error. If he had simply continued to caress her he could have made her give in sooner or later. But, instead of trusting to luck, he had begged. He had begged her, and he had promised her that he would not do anything more than touch her.

And, as a result, he had lost.

Because now she knew full well that she could control him. Now he no longer presented any great problem. He could touch her as much as he liked and she would always be in the driver's seat, calling the shots and setting the limits.

He would not seduce her. She had everything under control, had the whole situation in her hands, and she would not be seduced. Not by him.

He went on, begging, beseeching, and gradually she permitted herself to relax and to respond to his caresses. Her legs relaxed and his hands continued what they had been doing before. The fingers reached for the promised land.

When he touched her, his fingers soft and exciting through the very sheer silk of her brief panties, she shook all over with excitement. But now it was a controlled excitement. It could not get out of hand now, could not threaten her. She had everything the way she wanted it.

He touched her and she felt herself warming to him. His hands were so adept, so clever, and yet he was not going to succeed with her. He would arouse her but he would not conquer her, would stimulate her without winning her.

She was happy and sad at once.

Nancy and Dave were in bed.

They lay on their sides, facing each other. Their bodies were pressed together gently. Dave had one arm around his wife and he was gently rubbing her back and stroking her firm round buttocks. He tried to relax into the ritual of lovemaking but relaxation would not come to him.

He was afraid.

Afraid he would not be able to make love to her.

It was ridiculous, he told himself. He was a young man, just thirty-four, and she was also young, twenty-nine. She was even more desirable than she had been ten years ago when he had married her. No man could want a more beautiful woman to make love to. And still he was afraid of failure.

She kissed him, taking the role of the aggressor, plunging her tongue into his mouth. He forced himself to respond to the kiss. And his hands reached for her breasts.

She rubbed up against him and moaned.

He continued to touch her, murmuring little love words to her that fell automatically from his lips. And, gradually, inevitably, some semblance of desire came over him. His mind worked its own little fantasies and his body responded as much to them as to the woman beside him. Desire came—not persistent desire, not blinding desire, but a gentle desire that would be enough, enough to get this business over and done with, enough to stay her desires and let them both drift off to sleep.

He took her in his arms. In the very dim light he saw her lovely blonde hair spread over the pillow, saw the strange light of hunger in her blue eyes.

It began.

It started slowly and it grew. He moved and she moved beneath him. And, according to all the textbooks on the subject, they were doing very well, acquitting themselves nobly on the battlefield of love.

But he knew better.

If this were all there was to it, he couldn't help thinking the human race would have died out long ago. If sex held no more excitement than this, people would concentrate on more important and more enjoyable things. They wouldn't bother; lovemaking would become a vanishing art. People would prefer to watch bad westerns on television.

The inevitable intensity developed, the inevitable growth of passion that was physiologically inevitable, biologically preordained, and psychologically unsatisfying in the extreme. His breathing and hers as well became faster and more labored. His body and hers built up speed and passion, straining toward the inevitable goal.

A climax—

Then nothing.

Rolling away from her seconds later, he thought that perhaps it was significant that they could not bear to remain too close after it was at last over. Once the hectic pseudo-bliss had been painfully achieved there was nothing left for them. They had to be apart, alone.

She said: "I'm sorry."

He said nothing.

"I don't know what's the matter," she said softly. "I try, Dave. I wish I could be good for you. I really try. I don't know what's the matter."

God, he thought, *she thinks it's her fault.*

"I try," she said again.

"Don't talk like that," he said. "It was good for me."

"Was it?"

"Of course."

The conversation ceased there. She was good enough, he told himself. She could hardly be blamed for an inadequacy that was his and his alone. It was not her fault at all.

What had she done wrong? Nothing, nothing at all. She could not help one simple and elementary fact:

She was twenty-nine.

And he did not want a woman twenty-nine years old. Not him, not Dave Grantland.

He wanted a younger one.

About fifteen, say. Fourteen or fifteen or sixteen. That was what he wanted.

A young girl.

He tried to laugh but the laugh stuck in his throat. It was funny, all right. There was his wife, as beautiful and desirable a woman as there was in the world. And she was blaming herself because she could not satisfy her husband. Now how in the world could she blame herself for that? How in the world could she feel uneasy because her husband, God bless him, was abnormal.

A man who lusted after young girls.

A man who watched the high school girls on the street, stared hard at their budding bodies. A man who wondered how it would be with them, who thought about them and grew warm, who could only manage to make love to his wife by picturing her in the window of his mind as a fifteen-year-old girl.

An abnormal.

And she blamed *herself!* She didn't blame him, the one who deserved it. She blamed herself, as if there were something wrong with the way she made love, something wrong with her own performance and her own desires.

Funny.

He was the abnormal, the twisted one. And she was perfectly normal, yet she blamed herself.

Funny.

He wanted to laugh. But, although it seemed very funny to him, no laughter came forth. Tears tried to come forth but he stifled them manfully and slept instead.

Chapter 2

At twelve o'clock Joe Turley left the Gavilans' house and went home. Since officially Lucy King was the sole baby-sitter hired for the evening, she felt it would not do to have Joe on hand when Fred and Joanne Gavilan returned home for the night. Since they were due at twelve-thirty, she was careful to get rid of Joe by midnight.

The Gavilans actually returned home a minute or two before one o'clock. When they returned the house was just as they had left it. No evidence of Joe's presence remained. Lucy looked quite as she had looked when they left, her bra and sweater on once again, her lipstick reapplied, her hair neatly combed. They came into the house and she welcomed them, told them their child had been blissfully quiet throughout the evening, and accepted her payment for the evening. As usual Fred Gavilan made the perfunctory offer to drive her home and as usual Lucy demurred, saying that she did live just around the corner and it would probably do her good to walk. His offer was expected, just as was her refusal. She knew full well that he had already put the car in the garage. He always drove her home if it was raining, but on a clear night she always walked.

Joanne Gavilan asked her if she would like to have a cup of coffee with them. That, too, was expected, as was her explanation that she really ought to get home right away and get to bed. Some night, she thought, she would accept the cup of coffee and the ride as well. *That* would shock the hell out of them.

But that would have to wait. She said a gentle goodbye to Fred and Joanne, left the house, and headed along Aberdeen Drive to the corner of Lancashire Road. The house where she lived with her parents was the fifth one from the corner, almost in the middle of the block. She walked to it, took her key from her purse and let herself in. Her father was awake, sitting in the breakfast nook with a cup of coffee at his elbow and the financial page of the *World-Telegram and Sun* spread on the table before him. He had a pencil in one hand and was making check marks in the margins of the paper.

"Hi, honey," he said, looking up briefly. "How's the working woman?"

"Okay, Dad."

"The kid behave himself?"

"He didn't make a sound."

"Well," Howard King said. "That makes things easier, I suppose. Want a glass of milk and some cookies?"

"I don't think so," she said. "I raided the icebox over there. I'm not hungry."

"Your mother ought to pay you for baby-sitting," Lucy's father said thoughtfully. "Cuts our food bill. Homework all done?"

"All done."

"In that case you have a choice between sitting up and talking with your old man or going to bed. If you're smart you'll go to bed. Your old man's grouchy tonight."

"How come?"

"This," he said, pointing to the financial page.

"Oh."

"I've got the magic touch," King confided. "All I have to do is buy a stock and it goes down. But it could be worse."

"How?"

"I could play the horses instead," King said. "Go to bed now. I've got to think of something stupid to do. I have to be able to concentrate. You have to think hard in order to buy the wrong stock every damned time."

Lucy giggled. She leaned over, kissed her father goodnight, and hurried upstairs to bed. She showered quickly, brushed her teeth elaborately, and tucked herself into bed. She slept nude. Ever since a movie star had confided that she slept in nothing but Chanel No. 5, Lucy had dispensed with pajamas.

Then, lying in bed, she thought about the evening at the Gavilan home. She thought about Joe Turley, with warm hands and clever lips. And she thought about herself.

At the end of the evening she had done something which she had never done before. Because everything sexual was of enormous interest to her she reviewed it in her mind. It had been a new experience. New experiences were automatically interesting, especially when you were sixteen years old.

Very interesting.

They had been on the couch, of course. He had been touching her, touching the promised land with the interest of Moses. The parallel went further than that, as it happened. Like Moses, he was getting a glimpse of the promised land without ever being admitted to it. An interesting parallel.

"God," he had said. "Lucy, I can't take it any more. I have to have it."

"You promised," she said. "I won't let you, Joe. I told you before and you promised."

She had him there.

"Look," he whined, "you don't know what it's like with a boy. I mean, things build up, and if you don't release them it's no good. It's painful, like. It hurts. You can't walk because it hurts so much."

"Well," she had said. "But I won't do it. Go all the way, I mean. I told you that before. And I think it's nasty of you to want me to."

"You don't have to, Lucy."

"But you said—"

"If you'd just be nice to me," he said. "Touch me, sort of. You know."

His voice had a sort of whining quality to it that she found quite unpleasant. Still it seemed only fair to her that she do what he wanted her to do. While the pain he had described was in one sense exactly what he deserved, she did not want to see him suffer. Especially since she could relieve his suffering with no real inconvenience to herself.

"All right," she said.

"Thanks," he said. "I'll show you what to do."

He had showed her what to do.

Then it happened for him.

The peak of pleasure, followed by relaxation, limpness, and it was over.

He had thanked her profusely then, thanked her for "helping" him, and she was left with no desire for him, knowing that, because he had been so easily satisfied with less than the fulfillment of his desire, he would never be the one who would succeed in seducing her. He was a boy, a boy almost as inexperienced as she herself was.

And it would take a man to seduce her.

Now, with the memory relived and permanently recorded; she lay in her bed, unable to sleep. Joe Turley had succeeded in kindling desires that he had been unable to satisfy. His caresses had set her on fire and he had not been able to put the fire out. She lay there, frustrated.

Slowly her mind began to form pictures, sensual pictures. Her brain burned with soft and undeniable desire, and her own hands began to roam over her young body.

She closed her eyes and imagined that her hands were the hands of a man. A man, not a boy. A man who would touch her and stroke her and turn her from girl to woman.

For several long minutes she continued to touch her breasts, kindling little fires and bringing her pleasure.

She stroked her flat stomach, her gently rounded belly. She touched herself and thought of a man touching her, a big strong man who would do everything to her, a man who would not settle for less than fulfillment of his passions.

Lower.

Then she was touching herself, pitching her passions higher and higher with the skill of her own deft and artful fingers. The thought flashed through her mind that what she was doing to herself was wrong, sinful. But the thought was dispelled when she told herself that it was not her fingers that were doing those things but the fingers of an unknown and mysterious man.

More.

And she began to tingle pleasantly with a thrill greater than any Joe Turley had been able to bring her, a thrill greater than any she had ever experienced. She burned with a small gem-like flame, her heart singing, her blood feverish.

The passion grew, spread. She could remain still no longer and she writhed like a woman possessed by a devil, as she moved closer and closer to the edge.

Then the edge came into view.

And it happened for her. The pleasure was startling. And yet, as she lay bathing in the afterglow, she knew that pleasure was nothing compared to what she would feel when her man possessed her. Then it would be real, genuine from the beginning to end.

It would be very good.

She closed her eyes and drifted off to sleep.

Around the corner Nancy Grantland was having even more trouble falling asleep than Lucy King had had. And Nancy could not use her hands to put herself to sleep. She was suffering from a frustration similar to Lucy's and yet quite different. It was not a need for a man which was troubling her. She had just had a man.

She needed something else entirely.

She sighed heavily. Then she looked at Dave, his face relaxed in slumber. She had tried to be good for him, she told herself. And, although he had told her that it had been good, she knew that it had not. Not for him and not for her.

Once they had been good together. Once she had been so in

love with him that nothing else mattered. She had been able to fool herself, to believe that they were suited for one another, that she was a normal woman who needed only to love her man.

Once.

No longer.

Now she knew that she was what she was, that she could not help it, that all the confrontations with the mirror image could not keep her from facing, once and for all, her real self. She did not want to do this. She did not want to face the real Nancy Grantland, did not care to admit what she really was. The real Nancy Grantland was not very nice. They had a word that described the real Nancy Grantland. A word of seven magic letters. An unpleasant word. A word she knew too well, and a word she had hated for many long years.

A strange word.

A frightening word. A word with sinister implications, a word that meant all her attempts at normality were foredoomed to failure.

Seven magic letters.

A word:

Lesbian.

Somehow, now that she finally managed to say the word to herself, she was vaguely able to relax again. Not completely, of course—she was too keyed up and too disturbed for full relaxation. But, with the word out in the open forefront of her mind, it was much easier to approach relaxation.

It had been a long time. For more than ten years, ever since she had met Dave, she had steered clear of lesbians and lesbianism. At first it had been very easy. With all the love that she and Dave shared there was no real emptiness, no need for another woman. At times it had been hard for her to believe that she had ever shared a woman's bed, that she had lived the life of an abnormal girl.

When she did accept the fact, she thought of it as a stage, a stage on the road from girlhood to womanhood. But now every day she became more and more aware that lesbianism had been more than a stage. It was her real self, a self she had struggled to submerge forever through marriage to Dave.

But the self would not stay buried. The self jumped up again and again, making its presence known with unnatural desires that flowed through her beautiful woman's body time and time again. It was ironic, of course, that Nancy Grantland, so feminine in appearance, was not a real woman at all. Ironic but no less painful with its irony.

The funny part of it lay in the fact that she had never been a confirmed lesbian in the full sense of the word. There had been only one girl in her life—just as there had been one man in her life, the man she was now married to. But she could not forget that girl, or the way they had met, or what they had done. The memory was engraved upon her brain, etched into her mind forever.

The girl's name was Sondra Roscommon.

It had happened at college, of course. Clifton College, a small liberal-arts school in south-central Ohio. And it had begun in her freshman year.

Sondra Roscommon was her hall advisor, a tall, red-haired senior girl with a slender, streamlined figure and a full, sensuous mouth. Sondra was from New York, a sophisticated English major who, in Nancy's Midwestern eyes, was everything a woman could aspire to be. As far as she was concerned, Sondra was perfection personified. She made no secret of her adulation. She sought the girl out constantly—for advice, for friendship.

And then it happened.

It began innocently enough. She was with Sondra in the hall advisor's room at the far end of the hall. It was late. She had asked Sondra's help with a particularly difficult English assignment. Sondra had helped, and the assignment had suddenly become quite simple. When it was out of the way they remained in the room together, talking and listening to music. Sondra put a Bartok string quartet on her record player and the two of them sat listening to it. The harmonies seemed strange and discordant to Nancy's ears. But as she listened she began to find patterns in the music, beauty in the atonality, rhythm and music in what had been jangled noise.

For several minutes she was lost, out of touch with time and space, alone with the music. Then she looked up and saw Sondra studying her with a new light in her eyes.

"Nancy—"

She returned the look. And something began to move within her. She did not understand it at all, but it was something very profound and far reaching, something that involved herself and Sondra at once.

"Come here, Nance. Sit by me, Nance."

Like a character in a dream she got up from her chair and went to Sondra. They sat together on the bed. Sondra took hold of her hand and looked deep into her eyes.

Then Sondra kissed her.

It happened all at once. But later, when she looked back on the moment, she realized that it had been building up for days, weeks, maybe months. Then lips pressed together and tongues touched and the world quietly exploded.

The music played on.

They kissed like lovers, kissed for hours without stopping. It was to Sondra's credit that they did nothing more than kiss that night. Nancy, blinded completely, would have done anything. She was hypnotized. But Sondra refused to press her advantage. She contented herself with kisses.

Then, finally, it stopped. Sondra was the one who broke away, turning from Nancy. Nancy waited patiently, not knowing just what was going on.

"Nance—"

She waited.

"Nance, there's something I have to tell you and I don't know where to start. You have to know what's happening and I don't know how to tell you. I . . . I didn't plan this. So help me God, I did not plan this. It happened. I think it happened to both of us at once, but I can't be sure. I can't be sure about anything. I'm so mixed up I can't think straight, honey."

She did not know what to say or what to think. She was still lost, still unable to see clearly. Something was going on and she and Sondra were a part of it. But whatever it was, she was unable to understand it.

"Nance, you have to know what kind of a girl I am. And you have to decide for yourself if you're the same kind of a girl. You have to be the one to make the decision. I can't make it for you. It's up to you, honey. It's your mind that has to be made up. And

I want you to know that I'll respect your decision. Whatever it is, I'll respect it. I mean it, Nance."

She still did not understand. She watched, thoroughly confused, while Sondra stood up and walked to the bookshelf over her desk. She took a slim paperbound volume from the shelf and brought it over to Nancy.

The name of the book was *Strange are the Ways of Love*. The author was Lesley Evans.

"I want you to read this," Sondra said. "It's about . . . me, sort of. Maybe it's about you as well. I want you to read it, and to think about it, and to decide about yourself. You have to make the decision, Nance."

What decision? What was Sondra talking about?

But Sondra pressed the book upon her and smiled. "Go," she said. "Take it to your room. Read it. Think about it. Don't show it to anybody. And let me know what you decide. Take your time, but make up your mind."

She left and returned to her room and read the book. She finished it at one sitting, one painful but exciting session in which she discovered what kind of a girl Sondra was—and what kind of a girl she herself was as well. The answer was an easy one for her, one she did not have to sleep on. But she forced herself to take as much time as she could.

The next night, trembling, she returned to Sondra's room. She came in carrying the book in her hand. Sondra was waiting, nervous, wondering what her answer would be.

Her answer was a kiss so passionate that both she and Sondra were surprised by its intensity.

And then it began—a night unlike anything she had ever been

able to imagine. Sondra had been the teacher and she had been the most willing pupil in the history of the world. First they sat kissing for minutes that seemed like hours.

Then Sondra undressed her.

Her blouse.

Her bra.

"God, Nance! My baby, you're so lovely. Such breasts, Nance. You have the most beautiful breasts in the world. Did you know that? Did you have any idea how lovely they are? They are beautiful, you know. And I like them. I'm going to do things to them, my darling. I'm going to make them feel good. I'm going to get you so passionate you are going to scream your head off. You just relax. baby. You're going to love this."

Then soft lips—so soft, so very soft—

Like a woman.

God!

Like a woman making love to a woman.

Then Sondra, undressing her some more.

Her skirt.

Her panties.

"Nance, I love you so much. Nance, you're so pretty. So very pretty. Do you like it when I touch you here? Do you like this? I'm going to touch you all over. All over—do you hear me?"

Hands.

Lips.

It was an amazing night. Even the book had failed to prepare her for what Sondra did to her. No book could possibly have let her know what was going to happen.

It was wonderful.

Wonderful.

She spent that night with Sondra. It was a risk they did not take often in the future, but one they had to permit themselves that first night. Because they needed each other so desperately; ached for each other so fully, that neither was willing to stop at any point in the course of the night.

They made love until they were limp, exhausted, and then they made more love. Finally, ages later, they fell asleep in one another's arms and stayed that way until daybreak.

Then they awoke together and went to work once more, making fast and furious love that was a delight to both of them. It seemed magnificent—fresh and sweet and beautiful.

That was how it began. After that first night they were together once a day without fail. They would meet in Sondra's room, and there they would undress, touch, kiss, caress, and make love. At first Sondra had insisted on taking the initiative, but as time passed Nancy insisted on playing an active role, insisted on doing everything to Sondra that the older girl did in turn to her.

And, when her lips brought Sondra to fulfillment, she shared the thrill of the moment with the redhead, shared it fully, achieving a degree of satisfaction she had never thought possible from the sheer pleasure of another person.

The affair was a beautiful experience. It was more than physical. They were, as far as Nancy could see, truly in love. They would spend hours together, talking, whispering, and the whole world became something lovely for them when they were together.

"Remember one thing," Sondra once said to her. "As far as the rest of the world is concerned, we are perverted. Abnormal. Sick. We have to live a lie if we want to survive. We have to pretend that we are what they call normal—or else we're damned a thousand times over. It's not easy."

She had nodded solemnly. But, because she was very young, the truth in Sondra's words had sailed past her. She did not ever fully realize how unhappy Sondra was, how disturbed the lovely redhead was deep down inside.

It showed up that spring.

"In a month I graduate," Sondra had said. "In a month they give me a roll of parchment and I go away from you. Forever, Nance."

"Don't talk like that!"

"Why not? You'll find somebody else. I'll find somebody else. Life goes on."

"But—"

Sondra's eyes had flared. "What do you want us to do? Get married? Raise a family? Use your head, Nance. We're not normal people. We don't get to live normal lives. Not us. Other people do, but not us."

"We can be together, Sondra."

"Don't be ridiculous. You'll find somebody else. You'll cruise some nice little girl just as I got you. And I'll find somebody else, too. Don't worry about it, kid. That's how it'll be."

"But I love you!"

Sondra had sighed very heavily. "Sure," she said softly. "Sure. And I love you. And you're young enough to think that that's all it takes. I wish I could think that, sweetheart. But I can't. Too old, I guess. Too old and too experienced and . . . and too sick. It just doesn't work that way."

Nancy had refused to believe it. Quietly, persistently, she had made her own plans. She would leave school. She would follow Sondra wherever the redhead went. She didn't need a diploma herself, didn't need a college education. All she needed in the world was Sondra.

She never had a chance to try out those plans. Because, a week before graduation, Sondra died.

Officially it went down as an accident. Sondra's car, a high-powered little MG, didn't make a turn. It went over a cliff on Route 42. They had to take Sondra out of the car a piece at a time.

But it wasn't an accident. Nancy knew better. She knew the MG made any turn Sondra wanted it to make.

Not an accident.

Never an accident.

Suicide.

The accident had almost destroyed Nancy as thoroughly as it had destroyed Sondra. The blonde freshman was broken up completely, a nervous wreck. She wanted to follow Sondra to death, and she almost did, making a couple of tentative cuts in her wrist before she realized that death frightened her even more than life without Sondra did.

So she went on living.

And she returned to Clifton the following fall.

But she did not find a girl to take Sondra's place. It would not have been difficult to find such a girl. After a year as Sondra's lover, Nancy knew quite a bit about lesbianism and lesbians. She could easily spot the gay girls on the campus and could have had an affair at the drop of a skirt.

But she didn't want to.

For one thing, the affair she and Sondra had had was too deep and far reaching a thing to be replaced by a quick and shallow contact. For another, she was frankly frightened of getting involved with a girl. As far as she could see, such an involvement could only end tragically.

In death. Or sadness.

She did not want to die. Nor did she want to cause the death or misery of another girl. And so she vowed very solemnly to change herself. She would stop being a lesbian. She would force herself to become normal again. She would find a man and fall in love with him and marry him and have his babies. She would become a full woman, not a lesbian. A full woman with a man for a lover instead of a woman.

Sheer willpower did the trick. She met Dave Grantland and was surprised to discover that she was attracted to him. The attraction, as it turned out, was mutual.

The attraction ripened into friendship.

The friendship ripened into love.

The love turned into marriage.

And for ten years Dave had been the only person in her life. They were married and they lived together. Even the sexual adjustment came more easily than she had expected. She had thought it would bring her pain and misery, but love with a man turned out to be not painful but quite pleasurable, quite satisfying. While she never achieved the heights of pleasure that she had reached with Sondra, she worked to forget that little fact. And subsisted on what pleasure Dave brought her. She put Sondra out of her mind. Sondra was dead; so was the girl Sondra had loved. The new Nancy was a normal woman married to a normal man.

That's how it had been.

Now she tossed in her bed, unable to sleep, wondering just where she was going next. Maybe she was not lesbian at all. Maybe the relationship she and Dave had was just turning sour, or maybe she expected more from it that she had any right to expect. After all, they had been married ten long years. That much time could change things, could take deep passion and smooth it out a good deal.

Maybe.

She wondered. And, somehow, she knew that she was going to find out one way or the other. Something very deep and far reaching was on its way to her, something that would change the whole course of her life.

It would happen soon.

She wondered when.

CHAPTER 3

The next day was Thursday. It was an ordinary enough sort of Thursday. The weather was relatively pleasant in the New York metropolitan area. It was October, and October is one of New York's better months. The sun was out only briefly, but the general lack of sunlight was balanced by the lack of rain. The humidity was properly low and the temperature hovered in the high sixties, which was decent of it.

An ordinary Thursday. At seven-thirty Dave Grantland got up, showered, shaved, dressed, ate a quick breakfast of cold cereal with sliced bananas and milk, and hurried to catch the Long Island Railroad commuter train to Manhattan. At 8:15 Lucy King got up, showered, dressed, and bolted two scrambled eggs and a glass of orange juice, after which she hurried to get to Mataquois Central High School in time for her first class. At 8:45 Nancy Grantland got up, showered, dressed, and made herself breakfast of four buckwheat cakes with maple syrup, four strips of crisp bacon, a glass of orange juice and two cups of very black coffee, after which she suffered through one full hour of morning television before deciding it was high time she got out and looked around for a job.

An ordinary Thursday.

While he read the *New York Times* and waited for the Long

Island train to limp into Penn Station, Dave Grantland thought about the previous night and felt miserable over it. He thought that maybe he should try psychoanalysis or something. He obviously had to do something before he went out of his mind. When a mature man developed a compulsive yen for young girls, either he brought the yen under control or he engaged in some pretty asocial behavior. And the yen was not getting increasingly controllable. Far from it.

Every time he saw one of them lately, one of the young ones with her breasts newly grown and her body beginning to ripen, he began to quiver like a pimply adolescent on his first visit to a bordello. He hadn't quite gotten to the stage where he followed them down the street, but he had a dismal feeling that such a stage was not far off. You read about people like that in the papers, he thought. Guys who follow jailbait around and make a grab for it. Perverts. They lock them up and throw the key away. Was that what was going to happen to him?

God!

He folded up his newspaper and lit a cigarette, trying desperately to think straight for a change. It must have started somewhere, he told himself. He hadn't always been twisted sexually. Somewhere along the line something had gone radically wrong. Either there had been a distinct change in his life, or some force from way back had been dislodged.

But *what*, for God's sake?

He could not figure it out. The closest he could come was a vague, uncertain memory from childhood. He had been perhaps twelve at the time, thirteen at the outside. He had grown up in the country on a small dairy farm in upper New York State, and, like all the other kids his age in the area, he had gone swimming in a small creek a few miles down the dirt road from the farm.

One time there had been a girl.

He frowned now, trying to bring the memory into sharper focus. The girl—her name was long forgotten—had also gone to the creek that day to go swimming. They had arrived at about the same time, and for several minutes they had stood there, embarrassed, neither willing to strip in front of the other.

"I'll turn my back," he had volunteered at last. "Until you get in the water. Then you shut your eyes and I'll come in. No fair peeking."

He had turned and stripped. Then, when she was in the water up to her neck, she had called to him and he had stripped and joined her. They swam by themselves for several minutes, each careful to ignore the other completely. But he had been strangely aware of her presence.

Finally she swam over to him.

"You ever look at a girl before?"

He shook his head.

"Never play doctor or anything?"

"Never."

"Never saw what a girl looks like?"

Again he had shaken his head, vaguely embarrassed. And she had volunteered to show him. "You got to show me, too," she had insisted. "We'll show each other."

They climbed shyly out of the creek and sat on the bank. He studied her carefully. She let him touch her and he let her do the same to him. He had been frankly fascinated, exhilarated by the touch and sight of her budding breasts, intrigued by the rest of her.

She touched him, too, and he found it all very pleasant. If they had been a year or two older they might have wound up making awkward love by the side of the creek. But they were too young, and after a half hour or so of discovery and exploration, they gave up the game and returned to the creek, swimming once more. Then the afternoon faded into dusk and he dressed and hurried home for supper.

He shook himself. That was all he remembered—if he had ever seen that girl again, he had forgotten it. But that half hour of sexual awakening stuck persistently in his mind.

Was that how the whole thing had started? He wondered about it. Perhaps that half hour had been his first distinctly sexual experience, and as a result he equated sexual desire with extremely young girls.

Was that it?

He did not know, nor did he see what difference it made in the final analysis. Whatever the cause, he seemed to be stuck with the end result. He had a yen for very young girls. A shameful, abnormal yen.

And he had not the slightest idea what he was going to do about it.

The day was an ordinary one for Lucy King. Nothing at all of interest happened to her in the early part of the day. She did not run into Joe Turley until her seventh hour Spanish class. He had the seat across the aisle from her. And he seemed to be glad to see her.

"Hi," he said.

She looked at him strangely for a moment, then smiled.

"Can I see you tonight?"

She thought it over. It was, she knew, a reasonable request. They had become quite intimate the night before, and he wanted to see her again, probably to improve on the previous night's intimacy. By all rules she should want to see him, too, if only to show him that he couldn't get that far with her all the time.

But she didn't *want* to see him.

"I'm busy," she said.

"Baby sitting?"

"Uh-uh," she said. "Project for history."

"Hell," he said, "you got a little time, haven't you?"

"I want to get it done with."

"I'll come over," he said persuasively. "I had to do one of those last year. Maybe I can help you with it."

"I work better alone."

"We could have a little fun."

The expression *a little fun* seemed to Lucy to be as unpleasant a term for sexual activity as any she could imagine off-hand. She tried not to let her disgust show on her face but it was not easy keeping it hidden.

"I'm really going to be busy," she said. She wondered how he would feel if she told him that the history project had been finished for two weeks now. That, of course, was something that would never occur to him. He was one of those people who never did anything until the night before the day it was due. The idea that she would get the paper out of the way a good three weeks ahead of time would never enter his mind.

"Well," he said. "How about tomorrow night?"

She thought it over. Actually, she decided, there was no reason for her to avoid him entirely. He was a nice kid. He was a boy instead of a man, but he was a fairly nice boy.

"I can get the car," he went on. "And we could either go to a party or a drive-in. Whatever you want."

"Whose party?"

"My frat."

She didn't think a frat party would be too exciting, but it would be better than a drive-in.

"Okay," she said. "That sounds like fun. I'm sorry about to-night."

"Forget it," he said. "Tomorrow'll be better anyway. We don't have to get home early. We can really have a ball."

After school was over Lucy went home without even stopping along the way for a root beer. Her mother had some women at the house for the weekly bridge game and Lucy said hello to each of them in turn without paying much attention to any of them. She had a little homework and went upstairs to get it out of the way. She was a good student and all her homework was over and done with well before dinnertime.

When she closed the last book and capped her fountain pen she tried to decide just what she was going to do. It was quite a problem, she decided. She was pretty sure that Joe Turley wasn't going to be the boy who would get her to do it, but at the same time she was also pretty sure she was going to do it with some-body before too long.

For one thing, she was thinking about it more and more lately. That day in school it had been on her mind all the time, and the more she thought about it, the more she wanted to do it. There were a lot of things she worried about. The pain, for one, and the chance of getting pregnant, and the possibility that she would get a bad reputation.

That last point was an important one. Mary Lou Saygrantz had done it, once, with one of the boys in the school—and the rest of the school had known about it in no time at all. After that things got pretty rough for Mary Lou. The decent girls—meaning those who hadn't done it, at least so far as anybody knew—would not associate with her any more, all of them fearful of getting tagged with Mary Lou's reputation. The boys, on the other hand, flocked to her, every last one of them intent on getting some of what the first one had gotten. And the bad girls—the ones who put out regularly—were anxious to welcome Mary Lou into the fold.

Naturally, the poor kid hadn't been able to take that kind of triple-pronged pressure. Before long she had welcomed the friendship of the bad girls and the attention of the boys as well. The route from that point was directly downhill. It was hard to tell the rumor from the truth, but Lucy had heard some intriguing things about Mary Lou and was convinced they couldn't all be idle chitchat. According to one report, she had taken on the entire membership of one frat—thirty-two boys in all—after a stag party. Lucy tried to imagine being made love to by thirty-two boys, one after the other, and decided that any girl who could enjoy that sort of thing had something wrong with her. And to top it off, they said that while one boy did it to her the rest of them stood around in a circle and watched. It was disgusting.

That, Lucy decided, was the trouble. If you did it once, then you had to do it all the time. And she was by no means certain that she wanted to do it all the time. She certainly didn't want to turn into a tramp like Mary Lou Saygrantz. If that was "having fun," she could live without it.

What she needed, then, was a man who wouldn't tell anybody about it. That was another advantage of a man over a boy. Boys had to go tell the world just so they could feel superior, but a man knew how to keep his mouth shut. Besides, a man would know how to do it better than a boy would. That part was important. With a boy like Joe she might get pregnant just because he didn't know any better.

Then it was settled. She would go find a man and, if she liked him, she would let him do it to her.

But when?

Not tonight, she thought. She would stay home that night. And the next night Joe was taking her to the party. But Saturday night was still open.

Saturday would be perfect. She could stay out without having her parents worry, and she could find somebody who would do it properly. She knew just how to find that somebody, too. She would go into Manhattan, find a bar, and let herself be picked up. That was the way they always did it in the books she read. The man would pick up the girl in a bar, and then they would go to a hotel or something and they would do it.

It was settled, then.

Saturday night.

She smiled happily to herself and went to the bathroom to get washed for dinner.

•   •   •

Getting a job, Nancy Grantland discovered quickly, was not nearly as easy as rolling off a log. As a matter of fact, she learned, it was
difficult. Damned difficult.

Well nigh impossible.

To begin with, there were no openings on Long Island list-
ed in the regular New York newspapers. Long Island had a daily
newspaper of its own, a progressive journal known as *Newsday*,
but a careful study of the *Newsday* employment ads yielded nothing at all in Mataquois. Which meant that the only way for Nancy to land a job was to drag herself from one store to another until
somebody hired her.

Which was a pain in the posterior.

She went to store after store after store. Most of the storekeep-
ers simply informed her that they needed no help at the present
and would not be needing help for the foreseeable future. Others
dutifully noted her name, address and phone number and gave
her a don't-call-us-we'll-call-you routine.

It was disheartening. It wasn't as though she wanted a lot of
money or a golden opportunity. All she wanted was a job, something that would let her put in forty hours a week or so and pay
her something in return.

But nobody seemed to want her.

She was just at the point of throwing in the towel and calling
it quits for the time being when she noticed the shop. It was on
Guinevere Boulevard at the corner of Ashton Street, a small lin-
gerie shop with a window full of bras and girdles and slips. She
wondered why she had never noticed it before, and she decided
that she might as well give it a try. She was in the neighborhood

anyway, and there was always the slight chance that the proprietor could use a clerk.

She parked the Pontiac in front of the shop and walked in. A bell rang when she opened the door. She stood for an awkward moment in the empty shop, shifting her weight from one foot to the other waiting for something to happen.

Then something happened.

The girl who came from the back of the store was the most strikingly attractive girl Nancy had ever seen. She was a brunette, with her long hair caught up in a pony tail. The pony tail swished from one side of her head to the other as she walked. Her skin was pale white, her eyes very large and elaborately made up with dark eyeshadow. Her face was both beautiful and striking and Nancy could not help staring at her. She knew what she was doing, knew it was impolite, but could not help it.

The body was just as striking.

The girl wore a plain black blouse, more a man's style shirt than a woman's blouse. Two huge breasts made it obvious, however, that the wearer was not a man. The girl was really built quite spectacularly, and Nancy expected her breasts to pop buttons on the blouse at any time.

White slacks contrasted sharply with the black blouse, just as the girl's pale complexion contrasted with her very black hair. The slacks were also tight and the girl's hips were accented sharply. They were full, sensual.

"May I help you?"

The words jolted Nancy. It took her a moment or two to recover her mental balance.

"I . . . maybe," she said. "I'm looking for a job. Sales clerk, something along those lines. I thought maybe—" Her voice trailed off as she noticed the girl was studying her very frankly, her eyes taking Nancy in carefully.

"You want a job?" The girl's voice was pitched low. She talked slowly.

"That's right."

"Live around here?"

"In Mataquois. On Aberdeen Drive, just a few blocks from here."

"I see," the girl said. Nancy guessed her age at twenty-five, a year or so either way. "Housewife looking for something to do or what?"

"That's right," she said. "My husband and I don't have any children and it gets boring, just sitting around the house all day. I thought maybe if I could get a job—" Again her voice trailed off and she stood helpless, waiting for the other girl to say something.

The girl took out a cigarette and lit it. "Well," she said. "Funny thing is that you picked the right time to drop by. I had a girl here for awhile and she quit on me less than a week ago. Not that I blame her. It's hard for me to keep help, you see. This business is just about enough to keep me alive. People shop here when they need a bra or a girdle or a pair of stockings in a hurry. I can't compete with the department stores so I don't have any regular trade. Just people in a hurry. Enough to keep me going, but not enough to get rich on."

"I see."

"So if I hire a girl," the brunette went on, "I can't pay her much. Dollar an hour is as much as I can offer. Only time I can use help is from ten to four. Six hours a day, five days a week—not many women want to work for thirty bucks a week. Not when you can make double that sitting on your butt in an air-conditioned office."

Nancy found her voice. "But it would be perfect for me," she said. "You see, just a little money would be better than what I earn now. And I wouldn't have to get up early, and I could get home in time to make dinner. It would be perfect for me."

"Then you want the job?"

"Then I can have it?"

They both laughed at once. "Better tell me who you are," the dark-haired girl said. "If you're going to work for me, I'll have to know your name."

Nancy introduced herself.

"I'm Roberta Ryan," the brunette said. "Bobby for short. Bob if you've only got time for a single syllable."

A bell rang in Nancy's head.

"We've got a couple hours," Bobby said. "And business is about as slow as it ever gets. I might as well show you the set-up. Then you can start tomorrow."

By the time it was four o'clock and time for her to go home for the day, Nancy knew two things. They came to her not all at once but slowly, gradually. But she knew them for certain. In the first place, Bobby Ryan was a lesbian. That, she thought, was something she might not have known if she hadn't been a lesbian herself. The girl was a lesbian with enough intelligence to keep her hobby under wraps while she was working.

But she could tell nevertheless. There was something about Bobby, some subtle but obvious factors that, added together, made Nancy very certain of Bobby's sexual preferences. Bobby, evidently, did not notice the same factors in Nancy.

But she would.

Because that was the second discovery. The discovery, simply enough, was that she and Bobby were going to have an affair. It was inevitable, she decided. She couldn't look at Bobby without feeling strongly attracted to her. She couldn't look at the girl's lips without imagining the way they would feel on her body. She couldn't look at Bobby's breasts and hips without itching to touch and stroke and kiss.

It was going to happen.

It was, she decided, when she went home to cook supper for Dave and herself, only a question of time. Sooner or later Dave was going to call her and tell her he would have to work late. She did not know whether or not he worked late on nights when he called her like that, nor did she especially care. But, the next time she got such a call, it would be her turn.

She would make a pass at Bobby.

Nancy giggled. The girl would probably be astounded, but she would also be pleased. It was not hard to tell that Bobby was at least as strongly attracted to her as she was to Bobby. So, when Dave called her and told her he was going to be working late, she would surprise Bobby with a kiss.

Then they would spend the evening in each other's arms.

Her heart sang in anticipation. She could hardly wait. She whistled in the kitchen as she prepared dinner, imagining how wonderful it would be to make love to Bobby.

She burned inside.

•   •   •

For Dave Grantland, lunch hour was the moment of discovery.

He had lunch that day with Artie Merino. Artie was a heavy-set, balding draftsman in the art department, a man in his late thirties who talked a blue streak.

This time, for a change, Dave listened.

They were eating lunch at the Red Bull, a medium-priced restaurant on 48th Street around the corner from their office on Madison Avenue. The food was good—German food, sauerbraten and potato dumplings and red cabbage. But this time Dave hardly noticed what he was eating.

"Never saw a place like it," Artie was saying. "You familiar with the area at all? The west Twenties?"

Dave shook his head.

"Quite an area," Artie said. "Real weird neighborhood. Lot of Puerto Ricans, lot of Greeks, a few Irish. Nice place if you want a little fun."

Dave waited.

"But this one place," Artie went on. "Believe me, I've been to a lot of pretty exciting places. I was in the Navy, you know. That was before I got married, settled down. Well, I was in the Navy and we had a lot of things going. Girl in every port—that was no bull, believe me. The sailors always know what's going on, always get their share of it."

"About this place—"

"Yeah," Artie said. "A Greek place. A coffee house, sort of. You ever been down to the Village?"

Dave nodded.

"A coffee house, like I said. But not like the ones in the Village, not full of tourists or anything. It's a coffee house for the Greeks who live around there. You go up there and you see 'em sipping this strong thick coffee, reading newspapers, maybe playing a game of dominoes."

"That's all."

"That's it, man."

"What's so exciting about a batch of Greeks drinking coffee and playing dominoes?"

Artie grinned wickedly. "Hang on," he said. "I'm just coming to the point. You go in there, you see, and you take a table. By yourself. You just take a table and when the waiter comes over you tell him you want some coffee. Got it?"

"But—"

"Hang on a minute, will you? So you sit there and he brings over the coffee, and if you feel like it you drink it, and if you don't want to you let it sit there and get cold in front of you. And pretty soon this guy comes over."

"What guy?"

"His name is Kyros," Artie said. "A Greek. A big fat guy. He must weigh four hundred pounds, to look at him. Rolls of fat. And little beady eyes. You see that Sidney Greenstreet movie where Greenstreet plays this Greek spy. That's this guy. Looks just like him."

Dave waited patiently.

"He sits down across from you," Artie went on. "Kyros, this Greek, he sits down across from you. And he asks you if there's anything you can use."

"I don't get it."

Artie grinned again. "Anything," he said, stretching the word out. "Anything at all. You name it, this Greek can get it for you. He'll take you where you can get anything you want. And not too expensive, either. Not cheap, not cut-rate or anything. But not too expensive. Not for what you're getting."

"What are you getting?"

"Whatever you want. Believe me," Artie said. "Whatever you want. You want to take on two girls at once, Kyros gets 'em for you. You want two girls, identical twins, Kyros gets 'em for you. You imagine what it's like sacking out with a pair of identical twins? Both in the same bed at the same time? Both willing to do anything in the world you want 'em to do?"

Artie smiled triumphantly.

"Oh," Dave said. "Women."

Artie shrugged. "Women, boys, anything you want. But not just *women*. Special."

"Special?"

Artie sipped his coffee. "Some people have special tastes," he said, winking. "You and me, we're family men. We got our wives and that's all we need, you and me. But some guys have their own private kicks. Like for instance a guy enjoys it with a pregnant woman. You ever hear of guys like that? It's a fact. You want a pregnant girl, Kyros can find one. He's a sharp one, Kyros."

Dave was interested. Not in a pregnant woman—God in heaven!—but in what Kyros could get.

"Or say you're interested in something else. Say you want to beat up a girl. You know, like a sadist. Some guys, that's their kick. Kyros can find girls willing to get beat up on. Or he can find girls who will swing a whip at you if that's your scene. From what I've heard, you'd be surprised how many men get a kick out of being whipped by a chick. Me, I can't see it. But you never know what somebody's kick is going to be."

Yes, Dave thought, you never know. And Artie didn't know what *his* private kick was. Nobody knew.

But maybe Kyros could supply what he wanted. That would be better than driving himself crazy, better than following young girls down the street.

Better than what he was afraid might happen some day. Better than grabbing some innocent girl and dragging her into an alley and tearing her clothes off and—

"There's kicks and there's kicks," Artie confided. "Some guys, they don't want to *do* anything. They want to watch somebody else do it. Ever watch a show? I did one time in France. People making it, that sort of thing. They had some pretty weird acts, believe me. You want a show, Kyros can steer you to it."

"Sounds like quite a guy."

"You said it," Artie said. "Or suppose a guy likes young kids. Boys or girls, it doesn't matter a damn to Kyros. I heard of a guy who went to Kyros and Kyros put him on to a ten-year-old girl. Can you imagine that? Pretty sickening, far as I'm concerned. Making a ten-year-old kid do things like that. But you can get anything you want. Anything in the world."

Dave tried to conceal his interest. It was not easy. He was about as interested as a person can get.

"Of course," Artie said, "guys like you and me, there's nothing there that could interest us. We're family men. Got our wives. Nothing there for us. Our wives can take care of us and to hell with Kyros. Right?"

"Right," Dave said.

"But for somebody who's interested, you can do worse than look up old Kyros."

Artie lapsed annoyingly into silence and Dave tried to digest what the man had said. If Artie was telling the truth, a solution had suddenly appeared to a very pressing problem. If Kyros could turn up a ten-year-old, he could definitely find something around fifteen or sixteen.

Just what he wanted.

He closed his eyes and pictured a sixteen-year-old girl. Not a frightened, unwilling one, but one who was in it for the money, a sixteen-year-old hustler ready to do whatever he wanted her to do, ready to satisfy him one hundred percent.

It was fantastic.

"Say," he said, trying desperately to make his voice sound casual, "where does this Kyros character hang out?"

"I told you," Artie said.

"Tell me again."

"The west Twenties."

"Any special place?"

"Yeah," Artie said. "This café. A coffee house. I guess you would call it."

Dave tried to relax.

"But what the hell," Artie went on, grinning, "you don't really care where it is. You're a family man, same as I am. You wouldn't want to go there."

Dave said nothing.

"Would you?"

"No," he said. "Of course not."

"I didn't think you would. But I'll bet you got a brother, haven't you? A younger brother. Not married yet. You got a brother, haven't you?"

"Sure," Dave said. He did not have a brother.

"Just the way I figured it," Artie said maddeningly. "This brother, he could probably use a good time. You know. I mean, he's not a family man like you and me. Right?"

"That's it," Dave said easily. "He's just a kid. Doesn't have too much fun."

"That's what I figured."

Silence.

"And you'd like to tell him about this place," Artie prompted. "So he can have himself a ball. Right?"

"Right."

"Figured as much. Well, you tell him it's on Eighth Avenue and 27th Street. Got that?"

Dave nodded.

"Name of the place is Hassan's. On the second floor. You walk right up."

"Hassan's," Dave repeated, committing the name to memory. "Second floor. Eighth and 27th."

"You got it," Artie said. "Can't miss it. That is, your brother can't miss it." His eyes gleamed wickedly. Dave wanted to say something but there was nothing to say.

"I think he'll like it there," Artie said. "It's a fine place. Of course, I've never been there. I mean, I'm a family man and all. But my kid brother goes there all the time. Really wild about the place. You know how those young single guys are."

A most elaborate wink.

Later, alone at his desk, Dave wondered what Artie's private kick was. And he hoped he wouldn't run into the man at Hassan's.

Chapter 4

Thursday night was uneventful. Lucy King sat home alone, watching television with her mother and father and being quite bored by the whole thing. The bulk of the evening interested her not at all, but she did manage to enjoy the hour-long crime program, *The Untouchables*. The film concerned the activities of a Chicago mob importing prostitutes from Mexico and the efforts of Eliot Ness and his gang of untouchable agents to smash the group. Crisp dialogue and pleasant violence carried the show, but the high point for Lucy King was the idea of prostitution in the abstract. She sat in front of the set and wondered to herself just what it would be like for a girl to have intercourse for money. It was hard to understand just what sort of life it would be.

It was particularly difficult for her imagination to come up with anything conclusive in light of the fact that she had not yet had intercourse at all, for love or money or the sheer hell of it. But, since she had already decided that making love was fun, she could not see anything wrong with getting paid for it. *Turn your hobby into a profitable business*, she thought to herself. *Have fun and make money*.

She shook her head and sighed softly to herself. Maybe she would become a high-priced call girl and live in a plush penthouse apartment overlooking Central Park. She had read about high-priced call girls. It sounded romantic, exciting.

Then *The Untouchables*, which still sounded like it ought to be a program about the caste system in India, came to a close. So she watched a private eye ferret out a blackmailer while her mind gently turned to thoughts of sex.

Around the corner Nancy Grantland told Dave about her job. She tried to keep from sounding too excited while Dave tried to pay attention to what she was saying.

"Well," he said, "it'll certainly keep you busy. And an extra thirty bucks a week'll come in handy. Every penny counts, you know."

He thought for a moment. "Say," he said, "you better give me the phone number there. In case I get tied up at the office or something. So I'll be able to get in touch with you."

Nancy's heart sang. She hoped he would get tied up at the office in the very near future. Then she and Bobby would be alone. Together.

She gave him the number. He wrote it down carefully on a small slip of paper and tucked the slip into his wallet. "Good enough," he said. "If I have to reach you I'll call you there."

Call soon, she thought. *Call tomorrow. Call as soon as you can and tell me you'll be very very late.*

Maybe tomorrow, he thought. *Do I dare call that soon? But she won't suspect anything. And even if she does, she won't have any proof.*

•   •   •

Friday morning Lucy went to school, Dave to Manhattan, Nancy to work. The sun was high in the skies, the air warm and clear. A good day.

Dave worked hard during the day, straining himself to channel all his energies into his job. He had difficulty in concentrating at first, but after careful thought and strong willpower and two capsules of Dexedrine he put his mind to work on his job. The phone on his desk beckoned to him and he had trouble suppressing the urge to call Nancy.

Nancy, too, had trouble suppressing an urge. It was, however, a different urge entirely. The urge stabbed into her intestines every time she got a good long look at Bobby. The brunette was wearing slacks again, red ones this time. Her blouse was a man's paisley shirt with green and brown predominating. She looked good enough to eat, which was precisely the thought that kept crossing Nancy's mind.

Ring, she told the telephone.

She wanted to reach for Bobby, to touch her, to kiss her, to tell her that she, too, was a lesbian, that she, too, was very much interested in horizontal activity, that she, too, was gay as a jay and hot as an H-bomb test area.

Ring, she told the telephone. *Ring, you stupid phone. Ring, ring, ring. Ring and let it be a call from Dave and let us, for the love of God, get this show on the road. Ring, damn you.*

At seventeen minutes after three a large man in an office on Madison Avenue picked up a telephone and dialed seven numbers. A few seconds later an attractive brunette in Mataquois, on Long Island, picked up a receiver.

"Treasure Chest," the brunette said.

"Uh . . . is Mrs. Grantland there?"

The brunette covered the mouthpiece of the phone with the palm of one hand. "Nancy," she called. "Phone for you. Come and get it."

A blonde woman walked from the front of the store to the back room. She took the phone from the brunette, held the receiver to her ear.

"Hello?"

"Hi, honey. Dave."

"Oh. What's the matter?"

"Work's the matter," the man said. "Heaps and piles of it. The weekend rush."

"You have to work late?"

"You guessed it," the man said. "We're really snowed under down here. I'll be a long while."

The blonde took a deep breath. "I see," she said.

"I'll be late."

"How late?"

"Hard to say. Let me put it this way—you better not wait up for me."

"That late?"

"Could be."

The blonde tried to keep the unadulterated glee from coming through in her voice. "Poor husband," she said. "Say, if you call me and I'm not home, don't panic. I may go out and catch a movie. Unless you don't think I should."

"Why not?"

"Okay," she said. "I might, then. I'll expect you when I see you."

"Fine," the man said. "I'll be home as soon as I can."

Nancy held onto the phone for several seconds after he had hung up, hardly able to believe the words she had heard. He was working late, very late, and she would have the whole evening to herself. The whole evening!

She put the phone back on the hook, her hands trembling slightly. "Bobby," she called softly, "could you come back here for a minute or two?"

"What's up?"

"I want to tell you something."

"Come on out front, then. Nobody here. You can tell me out here."

"Please come in the back."

Bobby appeared, her face puzzled. She pointed to the phone. "Bad news?"

"My husband," Nancy said. "Dave. He called to tell me he's working late tonight."

"Uh-huh. You worried that it's just a story? Afraid he's got something going for himself?"

"No," Nancy said. "It's not that."

"It happens, you know. All men cheat from time to time. It's nothing to worry about."

"I know. But that's not it."

"What is?"

"I'm going to be alone tonight."

Bobby looked more puzzled than ever. Nancy looked at her, looked at the high breasts, the very slender waist. She looked at Bobby's hair. It was not in a pony tail today but in a severe bun on the back of her head. Nancy thought it looked very lovely. She thought everything about Bobby looked very lovely.

"I don't get it."

"Come here, Bobby."

The brunette approached, still puzzled, evidently getting a glimmer of what Nancy was driving at but unable to be sure of herself.

Nancy moved toward her. She was very shaky now, very nervous. If Bobby *wasn't* a lesbian, she thought hysterically, then she might as well take a razor and open her veins in the bathtub. It would be the end of everything. But she had already gone too far to back down now. She had to go through with the move, what ever the results should happen to be.

And, suddenly and impulsively, she kissed the brunette on the mouth.

To say that Bobby was surprised would be like saying that Death Valley has a fairly warm climate. The dark-haired girl was completely shocked. Her mouth fell open and her eyes rolled. She stepped back, totally unable to get a grip on the situation.

"That's right," Nancy said. "That's right. I kissed you. I know what I'm doing, Booby."

"This is nutty."

"No it isn't. I know what I'm doing. And I know you wanted me to. Didn't you?"

Bobby didn't say anything for a moment. She turned to one

side, found a pack of cigarettes and shook one loose. She put it between her lips.

"Give me one, please. I think I need it."

Bobby passed her the pack and Nancy took a cigarette. She put it in her mouth. Bobby scratched a match and held out the light. Nancy took hold of her wrist, leaned forward to accept the light, and the physical contact between them was positively electric. They could both feel it.

Then Bobby lit her own cigarette, extinguished the match with a flick of the wrist and dropped it on the floor.

"All right," she said. "All right, I'm not going to try fighting it. It's real, okay. You're not kidding."

"I'm not."

"How did you know? I didn't think it showed, Nance. You don't mind if I call you Nance, do you?"

She shook her head. Sondra had called her Nance. No one else had, ever.

"How did you know? Nobody told you. Nobody knows. I've been pure as the driven snow since I hit Mataquois. The only sinning I've done has been in Manhattan. Nice quickie contacts that were about as satisfying as they were meaningful. Quick pick-ups in gay bars and quick trips to bed. Then a nice subway ride back to the Island. How did you know, Nance? What did I do? What tipped you off?"

"I don't know."

"Sure?"

Nancy nodded. "I just could tell," she said. "I just felt it and I knew."

"Just like that?"

Nancy nodded. Her heart was beating a mile a minute and she was too excited to speak.

"It can happen that way," Bobby said. "They say it takes one to know one. But I'm one, and I sure as hell didn't pick you for a lesbian. Maybe I'm out of practice. But I wanted you, Nance. God knows how much I wanted you. I suppose that's why I hired you. I don't really need help here, not when you come right down to it. I hired you because I wanted you. I wasn't cruising you, you understand. I didn't dare make a pass at you. But in the back of my mind I couldn't help hoping—"

The bell rang.

"Damn it to hell," Bobby said. "A customer. They only come when you don't want them. You wait right here, honey, just wait here while I get rid of this damned customer. I'll be right back, baby. Don't go away."

Nancy waited, trying to be calm. It was by no means easy to be calm. Her heart was beating too fast and her hands were shaking too violently. She waited for minutes that passed like hours until Bobby reappeared.

"Fat old broad," the brunette announced. "Fat old broad with her tits hanging down to her knees. Wanted something that would make her look like a woman. I don't know how she's going to stuff all that worn out meat into the bra I sold her. Well that's her problem. Now where were we?"

Nancy answered her with a kiss. This time Bobby was not surprised, and this time everything was quite perfect. Nancy was amazed at the softness of Bobby's lips. It had been such a long time since she had kissed a girl. Bobby held her close and Bobby's tongue slipped into her mouth, touching, prying, setting her on fire. Nancy pressed the brunette close and their bodies touched. She felt Bobby's hard breasts press into her own breasts and she wanted to scream with sheer physical joy. She ached to take those firm breasts and kiss them until she drove Bobby wild.

The kiss ended at last.

"God," Bobby said. "My God."

"So long," Nancy said dreamily. "Such a long time. I don't know how I managed to stand it."

"Want to tell me about it?"

Nancy nodded. She sat down in a chair and Bobby pulled up a chair beside her. Then, slowly at first and then with increasing confidence, she told Bobby everything. She told her about Sondra, about their relationship, how it began and how it flourished and how it ended so painfully.

Then she told her about her marriage, about the emptiness of the whole affair. Through the whole recitation Bobby listened silently and sympathetically. When Nancy had finished the two of them sat for several moments without speaking.

"You poor kid," Bobby said finally. "One woman and one man in your life. God, I've had so many women I couldn't tell you how many. Too many, Nance. All this time I've been looking for the right one. Maybe you're her, baby. Maybe you're the girl for me. I hope so."

Nancy couldn't answer.

"So many women. And do you know that I've never had a man in my life? I'm a virgin, honey. Isn't that one for the books? Pure li'l ol' Bobby. Never had a man and never will. I'd die first."

Nancy sighed dreamily. "Tonight," she said. "He won't come

home tonight. We can be alone tonight. Just the two of us. We can do . . . everything."

"I'll probably have to teach you a lot. For one thing I'll have to refresh your memory. How long has it been? Ten years?"

"More than that."

"You've got a lot to remember. And a lot of new things to learn. I'll be gentle with you, Nance. I'll take care of you. I'll be good to you."

"I know."

"We can go to my place," Bobby went on. "I think you'll like my apartment, baby. It's a pretty nice place. And you'll be the first girl I ever brought there, Nance. The only one. And we'll be alone together."

Nancy couldn't bear it. She reached for the brunette and their mouths met in a kiss. Their tongues played games and, all at once, Bobby's hand was on Nancy's breast. Nancy's whole body thrilled with the touch as the brunette caressed her firm flesh cleverly and skillfully.

The kiss lasted a long time.

"Tonight," Bobby said.

It was a promise.

Dave Grantland ate his dinner without really tasting it. His dinner was a good thick steak in a good steakhouse on West 36th Street. But he was too excited to care much about food. In an hour or so he would be at the place Artie had described in such glowing terms. Hassan's. There he would meet Kyros, and God alone knew what would happen after that.

Hassan's.

Kyros.

He had a cup of black coffee, then took a pony of brandy to steady himself. He paid the check, tipped the waiter, and left the steakhouse.

Hassan's.

Kyros.

A taxi took him to the corner of Eighth Avenue and 27th Street. He gave the driver a single and told him to keep the change. Then he looked around.

The neighborhood was a cosmopolitan one. There were bars, juice stands, candy stores and delicatessens and laundries and grocery stores on Eighth Avenue. 27th Street was residential— five-story brownstones lining both sides of the street for a block in either direction.

Hassan's.

Kyros.

He looked around some more, looking now for a second-floor coffeehouse. It took him a moment, but then, on the northeast corner of the intersection, he saw the place. There was a red-brick building, the bricks a rust color now with the original color faded by time, and on the second floor, over a barbershop, there was *Hassan's* lettered on the fly-specked window in uncertain script. He crossed the street.

It was not too late. He could turn around, catch a cab, go home. He could be at Penn Station in no time at all; then catch the first train to Mataquois. He could forget about Hassan's and Kyros and pretend he was a normal man.

Pretend. That was all it would be. Pretending, fooling himself into a false world. He was not a normal man. Not by any stretch of the imagination. Once, perhaps, he had been normal. The time was long gone.

He opened a door and walked up a flight of stairs. He reached the top and opened another door and stepped into a large dark room. Two dozen small tables dotted the floor. About a third of them were occupied. At one table two men were playing cards, their eyes dreamy. At another a man slept while a cup of coffee cooled at his elbow.

Dave found a table. He sat down, waited. He looked around the room and felt the foreignness of it. He was an intruder, an outsider. No one was staring at him but he realized that they were all aware of his presence, guessing his identity, sizing him up. He felt very much out of place.

The waiter, a very old man with rheumy eyes and an awesome black moustache, came to his table and stood there waiting for an order. "Coffee," Dave said. The waiter shuffled off and Dave sat some more. The waiter returned with a small cup of coffee which was too hot to drink. Dave stirred it absently with a spoon.

Then he saw Kyros,

The Greek was huge. He was about five-eight, but his circumference greatly exceeded his height. And he *did* look like Sidney Greenstreet playing Dimitrios. He wore a seersucker suit. This only intensified the resemblance.

He walked over to Dave's table, his face expressionless, his eyes beady. It was impossible to guess the man's age. He was so fat he was ageless.

He sat down across from Dave.

Neither of them said anything for several seconds. Then Dave raised his eyes and regarded the Greek thoughtfully. "You are Kyros," he said.

"That is correct."

"A friend spoke of you."

"I have many friends," Kyros said. "I can do great services for true friends."

"I could be your friend," Dave said.

"You wish a service?"

"Yes."

"There are many types of services," the Greek said. "Many types. It is surprising how many services one can be required to perform. Could you perhaps be specific?"

Dave glanced around. "If we could go somewhere and talk," he said. "Some place private."

"This place is private."

"All these people—"

"They know when to listen. And when not to listen."

"You're sure?"

"Positive. You may speak."

Dave took a breath. He reached for a cigarette, took the pack from his breast pocket and offered it to Kyros. The Greek shook his head. He motioned instead to the waiter who brought him a plate of pastries, baklava. The Greek popped a piece of the sweet baklava into his mouth and it disappeared.

Dave lit his cigarette.

"You wish—"

"A girl," Dave said.

"A particular girl?"

He nodded.

"One who will do something special?"

"A special sort of girl," Dave said.

"So?"

"A young girl."

Kyros's face remained expressionless. "It can be arranged," he said. "How young?"

"Fourteen. Fifteen."

"It can be done. It will not be inexpensive, but it can be done. For how long do you wish the girl?"

"A few hours."

"Beginning now?"

Dave nodded.

"It can be done. Seventy dollars."

It was a lot of money. But Dave could afford it. It would be worth the money.

"All right," he said.

For a shadow of an instant the Greek looked surprised, as if he had expected a bargaining session. Then his face was expressionless once more. "Wait here," he said.

Dave waited. He sipped his coffee which was too bitter, and sampled the baklava, which was too sweet. Then Kyros returned.

"It is settled," he said. "The girl's name is Nephrida. An Egyptian. Fourteen years old. She speaks little English. Enough to do what you tell her to do. A pretty girl. Satisfactory?"

Dave nodded again.

"Seventy dollars." Kyros took the money, counted it, folded it and placed it in an outside pocket. He stood up. "Follow me," he said.

Dave followed him.

•   •   •

Bobby's apartment was very nice. The wall-to-wall carpeting was mint green and very thick. The paintings on the walls were original oils, surrealistic scenes that Bobby had purchased in Greenwich Village. The furniture was Swedish Modern, obviously expensive. The music on the hi-fi was, incredibly, a Bartok string quartet. It brought memories of Sondra.

The meal had been delicious, the wine subtle and fine. Now the meal was over.

It was time for love.

It began slowly. They sat side by side on Bobby's couch and they kissed. Their bodies pressed tightly together and their mouths were greedy.

Then Bobby's hands found the buttons on the back of Nancy's dress. One at a time Bobby opened the buttons. Her hands slipped inside and touched the firm skin.

Nancy trembled.

Then, effortlessly, Bobby unhooked her bra. Her hands continued to stroke Nancy's back and began to have a phenomenal effect upon her. Desire rose up within her and threatened to explode.

They moved apart. Bobby caught Nancy's dress in her hands and removed it dexterously. She took off Nancy's bra as well.

"How pretty," she murmured. "God, how very pretty!"

Then Bobby began to touch her. The skin on her breasts tingled with pleasure as Bobby's fingers—so cool, so soft, worked diligently.

"Kiss them—"

Bobby needed no second prompting. Nancy closed her eyes,

her body responding as the weird harmonies of the Bartok quartet shrieked in her ears.

Without stopping the kissing, Bobby removed her own clothing. Her lips remaining busy at Nancy's breasts while she took off her shirt, her bra, her slacks, her underpants. Earlier in the evening she had undone her bun and her hair was free and long and wild, just like Nancy's. Now, as Nancy looked at Bobby's naked body, she began to ache with desire.

Automatically she stretched out on her back upon the couch. Bobby lowered herself and their breasts touched again. But this time there was no clothing in the way. Slowly, tantalizingly, Bobby brushed back and forth over Nancy. Bobby's breasts were a little larger than the blonde woman's, but they were every bit as firm, every bit as lovely.

She did this for a minute or two. Then the excitement that she was generating in Nancy caught her up, too.

"God!"

"Bobby! Oh, Bobby, this is so wonderful. God, I'm a grown woman and I feel like a schoolgirl. You make me feel wonderful, darling."

"I love you, Nance."

"And I . . . I love you."

"This is good, Nance. You like this, don't you? You like what I'm doing to you, don't you?"

"I love it!"

Nancy could stay still no longer. Nothing had ever been like this, nothing she had ever experienced, nothing in the world. She had had two lovers in her lifetime, a man and a woman, Dave and Sondra.

Bobby was a thousand times better than the two of them put together.

She twisted and squirmed under Bobby's caress. Then she felt Bobby's fingers hook under the waistband of her panties. Slowly Bobby drew the panties down over her hips and thighs, over her calves and feet. Now they were both naked.

"Lie still," Bobby said.

"I can't."

"Lie still. Don't move at all. I'm going to make the world spin around for you, Nance. I'm going to do things to you. Just lie still and enjoy it."

"But I want to do things to you—"

"Later," Bobby said. "Later. We'll have plenty of time. First it's my turn. First I want to do everything in the world to you. So just lie still while I love you."

She lay still.

And it began.

"So pretty," Bobby purred. "I'm glad you're a blonde, Nance. You're so very pretty. All that curly blonde hair. It's lovely, darling. Beautiful."

A hand, stroking as gently as a summer breeze.

Then Bobby was kneeling before her, kissing an inch above her knees.

Higher, now.

Higher.

She wanted to scream at Bobby, to tell her to hurry up and *do* it, to get it over with before she went insane.

But she forced herself to lie still while Bobby kissed her, up the inside of each perfectly shaped thigh.

Higher.

"So pretty," Bobby said. "The prettiest thing in the world. No one on earth is as pretty as you are, baby. No one in the world."

The sweat poured off Nancy's face. The blood pounded in her head. She listened to the powerful throbbing of her own heart.

"It's so nice. So nice and so sweet. Are you ready, my darling?"

"Yes!"

"Are you, baby? Are you ready? Do you want me to do it to you now?"

"Yes! Please—"

A kiss.

A kiss where Nancy wanted to be kissed.

It was the most exciting thing she had ever known. It was magical, and she was alone in the middle of the air with nothing in the world for her but Bobby's magnificent lips. The world began to sail around her and Bobby continued to do things to her, spinning her higher and higher, sending her through time and space at the speed of light increased a hundredfold.

Faster.

Higher.

Deeper.

More intense.

It had never been like this before. She had never imagined that anything on earth or in heaven could feel so good, so wonderful, so divine. This was life, peace, beauty. This was the whole world wrapped up in a single all-illuminating shadow of time. This was everything there was, everything there could be.

Kisses.

More kisses.

Bobby's lips were hungry demons drinking ambrosia from the lap of the gods. Bobby's hands were raised high above her head, holding Nancy's breasts, squeezing them expertly, tripling the already incomprehensible sensations.

More.

More . . .

Another record, another Bartok string quartet, had dropped on top of the first. The music was wild and fierce and it surged through Nancy's blood. She could feel it in every atom of her being. Now it seemed to be coming not from the two speakers on the far wall but from all four walls of the room, from the walls and the floor and the ceiling. It dominated everything, merged with everything, and the world dipped and swayed.

Bobby kept kissing her, and the music kept playing, and Nancy knew it was going to happen. She wanted it to happen, needed it, and yet she fought against it, fought against it because she wanted everything to last forever.

She could not fight it. The forces within her were too powerful to be denied. The excitement was straining for a culmination, and such a culmination was inevitable.

Higher.

Still higher.

And then they were at the peak, the very peak, and time and space stretched out before them like a vast and endless plain. An instant, frozen in the middle of the air, was immortalized forever.

She fell into a river of happiness she had never known before.

CHAPTER 5

The building was on 29th Street between Ninth and Tenth Avenues. On one side of the building there was a small machine shop; on the other side, a six-story warehouse. The building was three stories tall. It was constructed of yellow brick and was falling apart quite rapidly. The interior was even worse than the exterior. The walls had obviously not been painted in years and what paint remained was cracked and peeling. The stairs creaked with every step.

Dave Grantland walked to the third floor. There were three doors on the third floor, one red, one yellow, one green. Like a traffic signal, he thought. And, following Kyros' instructions, he walked to the green door, opened it and stepped inside.

The room was in better shape than the rest of the building. An oriental rug covered most of the unpainted wood floor. A king-sized bed with a blood-red sheet on it filled half the room. There was a sink in one corner. That was the only furniture the room had.

But he barely noticed the room itself. The girl commanded his attention.

She was an inch or two over five feet tall. She was very young and very slender. Her hair was a glossy black and reminded him of Egyptian paintings he had seen many years ago. Her mouth was full and sensual and looked out of place in her very young face. Her eyes were dark, almost black, and shaped like large almonds. Her nose was straight, her skin very dark.

"I am Nephrida," she said.

She was wearing a silk wrapper, pale green and quite sheer. Her feet were bare. She stood regarding him thoughtfully; then she opened the wrapper and displayed her body to him.

"Do I please you?"

She pleased him. He looked at her body, looked at the lovely rosebud breasts tipped with tiny coral nipples, looked at the flat stomach and the girlish hips. He stared hard at her body and his mouth tasted as dry as dust.

"You are very lovely," he said.

She smiled shyly. She closed the robe and came toward him and he could smell sandalwood perfume. He returned her smile and began to undress. He took off his suit jacket and looked for a place to put it. She took it from him, walked to a door and opened it. She took a hanger from the closet and hung up the jacket. Then she returned to him.

He wondered if she was really fourteen. She looked even younger. He knew that Kyros was not a man addicted to the truth. If he had asked for a thirteen-year-old girl, or a fifteen-year-old girl, he would still have been provided with Nephrida. Not that he had any complaints. Not at all. But it was something to think about.

She smiled at him, the same shy smile as before. He removed his clothes and handed them to her. She walked to the closet to hang them up and his eyes followed her, focusing on her buttocks. They moved tantalizingly under the silk wrapper.

She returned. He was not at all embarrassed by his own nudity and, evidently, neither was she. She looked at him very frankly and he did not turn from her gaze. This surprised him. Even with his own wife he did not like to parade around naked. When he made love to Nancy—and for years he had done so often, eagerly and with considerable pleasure—he had always made love to her in the dark.

But he wanted the light on when he took Nephrida in his arms. And he wondered why that was. It was strange.

She led him to the bed and he sat down on the edge. She knelt before him and began to unlace his shoes. He watched her, his eyes on the top of her head, his nose inhaling the delicate fragrance of her perfume. And he thought about what he was going to do with her, and how thoroughly society would condemn him for his actions. A girl her age! He could go to jail for that. Jail? He could wind up in an asylum.

She removed his shoes, placed them together beneath the bed with the toes pointing out across the room. Then she took off his socks and tucked one inside each shoe. Service, he thought. Real service.

She stood up then and walked toward the light switch on the far wall.

"No," he said. "Leave it on."

She turned toward him, nodded briefly, and returned to his side. She sat on the edge of the bed beside him and he looked at her and realized fully how young she was and how old he was. It was hard to believe.

She smiled at him. And he pushed her wrapper back over her shoulders. She swept it to the floor and he thought that it was strange the way she took such good care of his clothes while she was so careless with her own.

Then he kissed her.

She threw her arms about him like a little girl throwing her arms around her father's neck. But she did not kiss that way. Her mouth had a curious flavor to it, a fascinating blend of innocence and experience. He drank deeply from her mouth, tasted the sweetness of it. His hands caressed the satiny skin of her back. Her breasts—young, small, firm—were crushed against his chest.

They did not speak. They stretched out on the blood-red sheet, lying on their sides facing one another. He looked past her at the wall with its peeling paint and cracked plaster. Then he looked once more at her and forgot the wall entirely.

She seemed to know intuitively that he wanted it to take a long time. He desired a full program of preliminaries before the commencement of the main event and she recognized this desire on his part. She lay very still, waiting for him to take the initiative, to show her what he wished to do.

His desire surprised him. It was intense, but its intensity was a new sort of urge. There was no desperation in it, no instant need. Instead he wanted to drink deeply the pleasure of her fine young body, to enjoy her as thoroughly as he possibly could. His hunger was unhurried, almost placid. He was in no great rush at all.

He was amazed how good it was to hold her. Sweet was the only adjective that cued describe the sensation. He bent his body to kiss her breast and the perfume was more potent than ever. His lips raced over her and she tingled with soft, gentle pleasure.

That was the way he wanted it. Not a full blown, passionate woman, hurrying him, driving him on. A girl, a beautiful girl-child, enjoying his caresses and accepting them, letting him lead her very slowly.

He liked that.

No rush. Plenty of time. Time to relax, to enjoy, to explore and to savor.

He touched her for a long time, perhaps half an hour. He examined every last detail of her body, first with his hands, his fingers, and finally with his lips. He was no longer interested in the rules of society, no longer caring in the least whether his actions were sane or insane, normal or abnormal, healthy or diseased. Such considerations were no longer relevant. They did not matter in the least. He mattered and she mattered; the rest of the world could go hang.

Then it was time.

She knew it. She stretched out on the red sheet, lying on her back with her almond eyes closed. She opened her arms for him, and she was ready, and so was he.

He took her. She was small, almost too small, but he managed, and then they were together. It was not like armed combat upon the battlefield of the bed. Rather, it was a mutual blending, a growing together of two bodies. She made small, subtle movements that thrilled him. She grew around his passion and her hands stroked his back with something that could pass at ease for love.

He was awed that it was lasting so long. He felt that he could go on forever without ever tiring. His heart bubbled with joy and his limbs were light, weightless. He planted a row of kisses up and down each cheek. He kissed her lips, her small nose, her closed eyes.

Then the crescendo. A flash of light, a blaze of color. The world swimming beneath them like a red sea. The sea opening up, swallowing them.

The top.

And peace.

He lay in her amps for several minutes, still with her. Then, very gradually, he left her and rested on his side. She looked at him. Her eyes were shining, her face flushed.

He thought that he ought to feel tired. But he did not feel tired at all. He was strangely rejuvenated as though he had received energy by the lovemaking instead of having dissipated it. He looked at her and saw freshness and beauty. He dropped an arm over her body and caressed her.

He knew that he would be able to make love to her once more before it was time for him to go.

In comparison, Lucy King's Friday night date was rather pallid and boring.

The party that Joe Turley took her to was not at all bad. There was beer to drink, which she more or less enjoyed, and there were records to dance to, and there were people to meet. The people were ones who did not much interest her, the records were rock 'n' roll, and there wasn't enough beer. It was, in short, a typical high school fraternity party, no better and no worse than too many others which she had attended in the past.

So she was bored.

Finally, after the party had been going on for what seemed like at least seven months, Joe found her and took hold of her arm.

"This is getting to be a drag," he said. "Why don't we get some fresh air?"

Fresh air, she thought, was a pretty convenient euphemism for sex. But sex was certainly better than the party, and Lucy was all in favor of it. She walked with him to his car. The car was his father's, a two-year-old Chrysler sedan. She sat next to him and let him kiss her a few times before he started the car and pulled out onto the road.

"I know a good place to park," he said suddenly.

How clever of you, she wanted to say. Instead she said nothing but moved a little closer to him and rested her hand lightly on his knee. Immediately one of his hands covered it and squeezed it. She felt faint stirrings of desire, on his part if not on hers, and it amused her and pleased her that she could have such an intriguing effect on a man. But there was a time and a place for everything, and she did not feel like doing that to him while the car was moving. Later, perhaps, if he was lucky and if she was in the mood. But not just yet.

She moved her hand away, and at least he had the intelligence not to attempt to replace it where it had been. He drove in silence, then draped an arm over her shoulder for awhile, which was sort of uncomfortable. He wound up driving with both hands on the wheel, which was better.

The parking place was not some secluded and romantic spot on the top of a mountain, or at the shore of a lake, or the bank of a river. Instead it was in the very middle of a large lot which builders had not yet gotten around to subdividing. There was a tree or two, and there was a vast quantity of ugly grass, and that was about it.

"Well," he said unnecessarily, "here we are."

"Uh-huh."

She wished he would just plain grab her and start kissing her and touching her. Then at least she would be able to lose herself in excitement and forget what a complete and total clod he was. But that would have been too much to expect. He had to prove to her that he had a poetic streak.

"It's a nice night," he said.

She didn't have an answer for that one.

"And you're very pretty. You know, you're a nice kid, Lucy. I mean you're fun to be with. I hope you don't think I'm just going out with you for what I can get."

"I hope not," she mumbled.

"And," he added, "I honestly like being with you."

That was the end of the poetry. Because with that momentous and earth-shaking announcement he reached for her and she came to him. He kissed her, which didn't do a hell of a lot to her, and he put his hand up under her dress, which did. It was the speed of the act which excited her more than the act itself. He was daring. But then, after a minute or two the hand withdrew and the excitement vanished with it.

They spent two hours in the middle of that field. The time was neither dull nor stimulating. It was fun, she had to admit—fun when he kissed her with great passion, fun when he touched her breasts, fun when he put his hand under her skirt. It was even sort of pleasant when she caressed him until he had his fulfillment and quit for the night.

But it just wasn't what she wanted.

What she needed, she decided, was a man. A man who would

take her quickly and effectively without playing games. A man who would dominate her, not a boy who teased around trying to "get all he could get" instead of just taking what he wanted. A man who would be bored by petting, a man who would demand and receive complete satisfaction.

For that reason she decided that there was very little future in a relationship with Joe Turley.

This reaction was quite the reverse of what Joe had in mind. The way he saw it, she would want to hogtie him emotionally as much as she could. Since she was far and away the choicest bit he had encountered in his career as a dungaree Don Juan, he was quite willing to be a little hogtied.

So, when the car was parked in front of her house, he made the natural gesture. "Lucy," he said, "let's go steady."

She didn't answer, and he decided that she must be flabbergasted at the generosity of his offer.

"I mean it," he said. "I think you're pretty great. I wouldn't want to date anybody else."

"No," she said.

He looked at her, not sure what she meant.

"I don't want to go steady."

"It wouldn't have to be, you know, official," he said. "We wouldn't have to put an announcement in the paper or anything, I mean. We just wouldn't date anybody else. Just each other. Like going steady."

She shook her head.

"But . . . why not?"

"I don't want to."

"Oh," he said. He thought it over for a minute or two. "I guess you don't feel you're ready for such a big step," he said. "I suppose that makes sense. After all, we *are* both pretty young. It doesn't pay to rush into things."

She didn't say anything. She felt like telling him what a stupid fool he was, but she decided that would be too cruel. He would find out in due course.

"But we'll go out a lot," he said. "And then, when we get to know each other better, then we'll be ready to think about going steady."

To hell with him. "I don't want to go out with you a lot," she said, surprising herself with the directness and intensity of her statement. "I don't even want to go out with you a little," she went on.

He stared.

"I don't want to go out with you at all," she concluded. "I don't *like* you. I don't like *being* with you. I don't like anything *about* you."

And she swept out of the car and up the path to her door, leaving him behind, curiously baffled, curiously hurt, and, of course, curiously curious.

She hurried into the house, up the stairs. In her room she undressed and got into bed. Her head sank into her pillow and she thought about Joe Turley and how cruel she had been to him. Well, he would get over it. And it was better all at once than a little at a time.

This way he would get over her. Otherwise he would keep annoying her for dates, keep trying to further a relationship which had no future as far as she was concerned. This way she was rid of him permanently. And glad of it. He was a nuisance.

Tomorrow.

She sighed. Tomorrow she would find a real man. She would go to Manhattan, after telling her mother some story or other. She would go to a bar somewhere around Times Square and she would wait for Something To Happen. Eventually something would happen. And then she would find out what she had been missing.

Poor Joe, she thought. He would never know what he could have had if only he had been more of a man and less of a boy. He had really managed to excite her once or twice, and with a little effort on his part he could have had her dress up in the back seat of his father's Chrysler. But he had been too stupid about the whole thing.

Suddenly she giggled to herself. He would probably try to figure out why she had told him she didn't like him. And she knew the answer he would come up with.

He would think it was because he tried to get too much.

And that was funny. It was just the reverse, and he would have the whole thing upside-down and inside-out, completely and totally balled up.

It was funny. So funny that she could barely keep from laughing aloud.

She giggled some more. Then, abruptly, she stopped giggling, closed her eyes and slept.

Lucy was the last of the three to get home that night. The first home was Nancy Grantland, at nine-thirty, and the second was Dave, at a quarter to twelve.

Nancy came home with her eyes shining, her skin glowing, and her spirits soaring. She and Bobby had never gotten up from the couch once they had started. They had spent the whole night there, rolling savagely in one another's arms, and no experience had ever been so exciting for Nancy. She still tingled from the memory of it.

It was fantastic.

The pleasure that Bobby brought her was only a part of it. There was something else that was equally wonderful, equally remarkable, equally valuable. And that was the pleasure that she brought Bobby. When she was doing the things to Bobby that the long-haired brunette had done to her; her own joy had been doubled and tripled.

That, she decided, was what love really meant. Giving and receiving, with both facets of the relationship equally pleasurable to both parties.

Love.

I'm in love with another woman, she thought. *Isn't that hysterical?*

And, she thought, that was what made the difference. Love. Without it, her affair with Bobby would be no more significant than the affairs Bobby had spoken of, the quickie contacts with casual Village pick-ups. Fortunately, their love transformed the physical into something almost spiritual. It made everything they did something good, something clean, something praiseworthy. It changed what was traditionally an abnormal act into something that seemed to her to be normal. Making a lesbian love sound like the end of the world.

But that was exactly what it was. The end of one world, a world composed of boredom and nausea and the ever persistent feeling that she was only half alive. And the beginning of another world, a world of beauty and freedom and happiness.

A new world.

Now I'm an explorer, she thought. *Stout Cortez silent upon a peak in Darien. God above.*

Now that the affair had been changed from a dream into an accomplished fact, she would not have to wait for a call from Dave in order to lure Bobby. Now, with the preliminaries out of the way, they could have each other whenever they wanted. They were set now. Everything was rolling smoothly, ready to go, and any time they wanted each other they could close the store for an hour, hang up an out-to-lunch sign, and dine on rare and luscious food in the back room of the shop. They could steal an hour here and an hour there and they could be together, their bodies merging into one, giving and receiving the sweetest pleasure either of them had ever dreamed of.

Pleasure.

Fulfillment.

Happiness.

And yet, unfortunately, everything was not coming up roses. No matter how happy she was, there was something in the way to keep her happiness from enveloping her completely. That something, logically enough, was her husband.

That was the problem.

As things stood, she wanted to be with Bobby all the time, to spend every night in the soft warm circle of her arms. But obviously she could not do this. She was married to Dave. She lived with him, shared his home and his life as she wanted to share the home and life of Bobby.

What was she going to do? The first thing she thought of, inevitably, was divorce. But divorce, while a handy, convenient solution, was hardly a cure-all. For one thing, she liked Dave. She even loved him a little, although her love was nothing like the love she bore for Bobby. She did not want to hurt him.

And there was no question in her mind that divorce would hurt him terribly. The mere knowledge that she no longer loved him would be enough to crush him completely. She knew how deeply in love with her he was and she didn't want to make him feel bad.

But what other way was there?

None.

There were other things wrong with divorce. The way things stood, with her married to Dave, she had the pleasure of Bobby's body without the community scorn that would descend upon her if the facts of their relationship were known. She had the game without the name, and she sort of liked it that way.

Because, no matter how firmly convinced she was of the normality and naturalness of their relationship, she knew that society would see it differently. She would be an outcast, a misfit, a pariah—and she knew that this would not be a pleasant fate.

If she divorced Dave, the world would know why. Little by little and bit by bit the world would find out about the secret life of Nancy Grantland.

And that would be hard to take.

She sighed heavily. Where there was a will, she thought, there was generally a way. And somehow or other she would find the way. What she and Bobby had done had been too good to forget, too wonderful to abandon. Someway or other they would find a way to work things out.

They had to.

Dave Grantland, strangely enough, was filled with more or less the same thoughts as his lovely wife. He, too, had had a fantastic experience that evening.

The girl, Nephrida, had been amazing. The striking combination of innocence and experience had been precisely what he had been waiting for all along. And, when he had left her for the train ride back to Mataquois, he was beset by an unfamiliar combination of elation and depression.

The memory was sheer elation. The memory of the first time, so sweet, so gentle, so perfect from beginning to end. The memory of the second time—faster, more furious, but still controlled, still ideal.

And the memory of the third time. The mere fact of the third time was remarkable in itself. He had not made love to a woman three times in one night since he and Nancy had celebrated their wedding night. Now, ten years older, he had matched that record in the space of two and a half hours.

Extraordinary.

Magnificent.

Nephrida herself had been magnificent and extraordinary enough. But he was not foolish enough to attribute too much of the glory of the evening to the girl involved. He knew better. It was partially the girl and partially the simple fact that she *was* a girl—that she was very young and very fresh. Nephrida had been fantastic, but any girl would have done almost as well.

So that much was fine. The night had been great, worth three or four times the price. Worth any amount of money, because its pleasures could not be measured in money.

That much was fine.

But the problem, the real headache, was where in the world he was going to go from there.

The natural answer, of course, was to go to Nephrida or a girl very much like her whenever the urge came upon him. This, sad to say, was not a particularly workable solution. In the first place, the urge was very likely to come upon him at the rate of once a day. And seventy dollars a day was a good deal more than he earned.

But, even if he could live happily with one fling a week, he could not afford the expense. It was simply out of the question, and that made things rough.

He lit a cigarette and tried to concentrate. He could divorce Nancy, he thought. And his objections to that one were, strangely enough, much the same as her own arguments against divorcing him had been. He was convinced that she was so much in love with him that she would crack wide open if he left her. He liked her—she had been a good wife to him—and he did not want to hurt her.

And that wasn't all. Even if he got a divorce it wouldn't entirely solve things.

There would still be the expense. There would still be the fear of discovery, with the entailed fears of ostracism, jail, a number of unhappy punishments which society often reserves for those who deviate from its norms.

So there was no answer.

He smoked, drawing deeply on his cigarette, taking the smoke far into his lungs and exhaling a long thin column that rose lazily to the roof of the car. He tried to think and his thoughts refused to take proper shape. No matter how he added things up they came out wrong. No matter how he worked to get the total picture, the pieces refused to fit in place. There was always something out of joint.

He let his mind relax instead into the enjoyable channels of memory. Nephrida. Fourteen years old. Five feet two inches tall, jet black hair that smelled of sandalwood, soft-firm breasts just the right size for his hands, flat stomach, small straight nose, almond-shaped dark eyes, pert taut buttocks, warm tender thighs—

Nephrida.

He remembered everything about her. And this memory, combined with the fact that almost any girl her age would have done almost as well, was enough to drive him out of his mind.

What next?

There was, he realized with something of a start, one unique possibility. It was so far fetched that he didn't even want to bother thinking about it. It would never happen, not in a million years.

But if it did—

If it did, all his problems were over.

All he needed, he decided, was a mistress. A voluntary mistress. A girl fourteen or fifteen or sixteen—or even seventeen; he would stretch a point—who would love him simply because she wanted to.

A young mistress.

It was an impossible notion, but at the same time it was a notion that embraced so completely what he needed that he could not put it out of his mind. A girl who would be there whenever he needed her, ready to do whatever he wanted her to do. A young girl—a girl who would love him forever.

That was all.

Just the impossible.

He laughed in spite of himself. It was ridiculous. No young girl wanted to sleep with anybody, much less an older man. Not so old, really, but far older than the girl in question. It would be easy enough to have a mistress—there were women all over the place just dying to be asked.

But very few of them were fourteen years old. Or fifteen or sixteen or seventeen.

He dropped his cigarette to the floor of the car and ground it out under his heel. A few seconds later he shook another cigarette loose from the pack, popped it into his mouth, and lit it.

The train rolled on.

He got home, finally. He walked from the train platform to his own house on Aberdeen Drive, used his key on the front door and walked in. Nancy was waiting up for him and he was strangely glad to see her. He felt guilty—so much so that he never noticed the guilt in *her* eyes.

He told her about the pile-up of work at the office; and she listened sympathetically. Then she told him about the movie she had seen, a Civil War film entitled *A Sound of Distant Drums*, and he listened, with interest.

They went to bed and both fell asleep at once.

Chapter 6

John Gardner was a man with one interest only. This interest was, simply enough, making love. He did not want to make money, to get married, to raise children or dogs or tropical fish. He did not want to paint pictures or write books or sculpt statues. He did not want to sing or act or dance.

He wanted to make love.

There was a fairly good explanation for all this. Jeff's father, Brad Gardner, had made an incredible amount of money by the simple expedient of loaning a little money to a wildcat oil driller named Ben Brown. Ben Brown had hied himself off to Texas where he had brought in, one after the other, three of the most productive wells in the most productive state in the nation. Then, when Ben Brown returned to New York, Brad Gardner pointed to the fine print in their contract. Ben Brown was suddenly out on his rear and Brad Gardner was the proud owner of three of Texas's finest oil wells.

The wells still gushed forth. But five years ago he had been considerate enough to steer his deluxe fishtail Cadillac into another man's old Ford. Nobody survives a head-on collision when the combined speed of the two cars involved exceeds one hundred miles an hour. Since Brad Gardner was going one hundred miles an hour all by his lonesome and since the Ford contributed another forty miles an hours to the total score, nobody got out of either car alive.

The occupant of the Ford went through his own windshield. He also went through the windshield of the Cadillac, and they finally took him away in three pieces.

Brad Gardner took the steering wheel through the chest. Not just the steering column. The whole wheel.

Rose Gardner, Brad's wife and Jeff's mother, had insisted on safety belts as part of the car's equipment. She had read somewhere that safety belts could cut accident fatalities by more than half. She was taking no chances. And, as a result, they found her right there in her seat, belt fastened, body strapped in very neatly.

There was only one thing wrong. Her pretty head was in the back seat of the car, severed from her body by a piece of flying glass. Her hair was neatly combed, her face relaxed in death.

And so, at the age of twenty-three, Jeff Gardner had been endowed with a multitude of worldly goods. He had a town house—a four-story brownstone on East 63rd Street just east of Park Avenue which was sumptuously furnished and occupied solely by Jeff Gardner. He had a Mercedes-Benz 300SL, the finest sports car in the world. He had an extensive and expensive wardrobe.

And, because of the fantastic productivity of the three wells and the generous twenty-five percent depletion allowance which the government in its infinite wisdom had seen fit to grant unto all oilmen, he had an income after taxes slightly in excess of one hundred thousand dollars a year.

This sort of thing can stifle ambition. It is a rare individual indeed who, when faced with absolute security, incredible wealth, and no near relatives at all, can be ambitious, dedicated, or whatever. And Jeff Gardner, although rare enough in some respects, was not that rare.

Jeff had been something of a rake even when Rose and Brad Gardner remained among the living. At the age of thirteen he had managed the seduction of the maid, a feat rendered simple by the fact that Brad Gardner had hired the maid simply so that Jeff could seduce her.

At the age of fifteen he raped a girl. It was just that—rape—and it had taken three thousand dollars of Brad Gardner's money to squash the charge and the attendant publicity.

At the age of twenty-one, after having been expelled from three colleges, Jeff was one of New York's leading and most notorious playboys.

At the age of twenty-three, when Rose and Brad went to their just rewards, he was rich. And, by the time he was twenty-eight, he had settled permanently on his true vocation. He would do everything, everything sensual, and he would spare nothing to achieve the ultimate.

Jeff went far afield in his pursuit of pleasure. Occasionally, when nothing better presented itself, he would call up a professional and have her spend the night. But despite the technical proficiency of such a partner, there was invariably something basic that was lacking. The chase was missing, the enthusiasm of seduction, and as a result he preferred to "roll his own"—to find his own partners and introduce them by himself to the arts of which he was an acknowledged master.

Now, on a Saturday night in September, Jeff Gardner was sitting in the Robin's Roost. The Robin's Roost was a bar on Third

Avenue in the Fifties. It was a special sort of bar. There was no entertainment. The drinks were quite expensive. The Robin's Roost was fashionable, but only among a certain set of people.

People like Jeff, generally. People looking for pick-ups of one sort of another. Homosexuals, occasionally; lesbians, occasionally. But, for the most part, men looking for women and women looking for men.

Jeff sat at a table and nursed a daiquiri. He had been at the Robin's Roost for over an hour and nothing suitable had presented itself to his eye. A man had approached him, a bleached-blond man with tight pants, mascaraed eyes and, incredibly, false breasts. Jeff had not been interested. He wanted a woman, and the women in the Roost that evening were either ones whom he had had once and who were not worth a second round or women whom he did not want to have at all, either because of their age or their looks.

He filled his expensive pipe with expensive and highly aromatic tobacco and lit it with a wooden match. He sipped again at the daiquiri. He was bored, and boredom was one thing which genuinely annoyed him. When you have an income of over one hundred thousand dollars a year after taxes, you do not expect to be bored.

Jeff sighed. It was still early, but he preferred to begin an evening as early as possible. And if nothing happened soon he would leave the Robin's Roost. In fact, he decided, if nothing happened before his daiquiri was finished, he would get the hell out of the bar and head for greener pastures. There was a fine place in Harlem where he had been planning on going for weeks. Tall high-yellow girls with vivid imaginations. Prostitutes, unfortunately, but good ones. And an evening spent with them would be much better than an evening wasted at the Roost.

He looked up then, holding his pipe in one well-manicured hand, and at that moment the front door of the Robin's Roost opened, tentatively, slowly.

Then the girl walked in.

She was not a girl Jeff had seen before. And she was not a girl dressed for the Robin's Roost. She was wearing a skirt and a sweater, amazingly enough, and although such attire was hardly de rigueur for the Roost, the sweater was so tight and the skirt so insinuating that she could not look out-of-place in it wherever she happened to appear. She had a good face and a good body and Jeff Gardner was interested. Definitely interested.

He looked at her until she got around to returning his glance. His eyes made a quick pass at her. He smiled.

And she walked over to his table.

"Sit down," he suggested.

She sat down across from him.

"A drink?"

"Whatever you're having."

Jeff turned, caught the bartender's eye, held up two fingers and pointed to his glass. The bartender hurried. He brought two daiquiris to their table, set one before Jeff and the other before the girl.

They clinked glasses.

They sipped their drinks.

"What's your name?"

The girl told him her name.

"And what do you do?"

"Not much yet," the girl said. "I'm a virgin."

The girl of course, was Lucy King. Her candid confession of her unsullied state was prompted primarily by an overwhelming desire to get her cards on the table as quickly as possible. She was beginning to get quite nervous. The Robin's Roost was the fourth bar she had been to, and it was the first bar in which anybody had even bothered to speak to her.

She was beginning to feel that it was damned difficult to get picked up in Manhattan. So, when Jeff caught her eye and bought her a drink, she was impatient. He was attractive, well-bred, and he looked experienced. He also was a man, which was nice. A man instead of a boy. And he seemed to be interested in her. So she did not want to waste time.

When she told him that she was a virgin, Jeff's mind worked automatically. There were three possibilities. One: she was lying. But he doubted this. Two: she was a professional virgin, desirous of retaining her station. Three: she was an impatient virgin who wanted nothing so much as to get thoroughly loved.

"A virgin?"

She nodded.

"Saving it for your husband?"

"No," she said.

"For your true love?"

"No."

"What then?"

"For anybody who's man enough to take it," she said. "You, for instance. Would you like to make love to me?"

Jeff smiled gently. The classification now was obvious. Lucy was an impatient virgin, a very impatient virgin, and she was ready for the big step. All thoughts of the very fine place in Harlem left Jeff's head at once. He knew just what he wanted—a full-scale two-person orgy, a proper initiation of this impatient virgin into the mysteries and delights of love.

That meant that they would go to his house. It meant that he would spend several hours with her, and that he would introduce her to as many forms of love as he possibly could. He pushed his glass aside, not wanting to have any more of the daiquiri. Alcohol could limit a man's virility. Jeff wanted to be as virile as he possibly could.

But first he had to get everything settled in advance. Let the girl know who was going to be boss in their affair. That much was imperative.

"You'll have to do everything I tell you to do," he said. "I mean everything."

"Fine."

"Everything," he repeated. "And you won't be able to back out. Once we leave this hole together I'm the boss. No two ways about it."

She nodded solemnly.

Abruptly he stood up. "Let's go, then," he said. "My car's just outside." He walked out without paying for the drinks, knowing the bartender would put them on his tab. When he was outside he knocked the ashes out of his pipe and put it in the inside pocket of his tweed jacket. Then he took Lucy by the arm and led her to the Mercedes.

•   •   •

Nancy was going out of her mind. Saturday night, traditionally, was an occasion for the Grantlands and the Blackstones to play family bridge. This particular Saturday, however, was one which the Blackstones spent out of town. As a result, the Grantlands were spending a quiet evening at home.

And Nancy was simmering. Because if there was one thing she did not want, it was a quiet evening at home. She wanted a nice noisy evening with Bobby.

Instead, what she got was a quiet evening at home.

Dave was reading in his den. This made it a particularly quiet evening at home. Generally when he sat around reading he did so in the living room. This at least minimized the sensation of loneliness, even though his company was hardly what she wanted. But now, with him in his den and the den door firmly shut, she was left completely to herself.

And so she was in the living room. The television had been forcibly silenced, the doors closed over its face. She walked to the stereo unit, another of suburbia's finer status symbols, and studied it thoughtfully. She had never been especially sold on stereo even before they got their set and now liked it not at all. As far as she was concerned, hi-fi was just as good, a hell of a lot cheaper, and far more convenient. If there was any great sound difference between the two, she couldn't hear it. The system cost a fortune and the records they had to buy to feed it cost a dollar more than regular records.

Another delight of stereo lay in the fact that you had to sit in one particular position when you listened to it. If you wandered around the room, you distorted the sound balance and thus heard a different sort of sound from different parts of the room. Interesting, she thought, but not especially practical. Sort of useless, when you stopped to think about it.

Listlessly she walked to the record cabinet and thumbed through the stack of long-playing discs. There was nothing she really wanted to hear—but then there was nothing she really wanted to do, either, so she couldn't be too choosy. She kept rambling through the record collection until she came to a record that she hadn't known they owned.

It was Bartok's fifth string quartet, performed by the Vegh Quartet. She stared hard at the record, then removed it from the stack, slipped the record free from the jacket and popped it onto the turntable. She let the machine warm up for a few seconds. Then she threw the reject lever and the tone arm stood up, saluted, and set itself gently down upon the record.

She stepped back from the player, stepped back hesitantly, and found a chair placed in the right position for stereo listening. By all rules she would get the proper sound balance there, and the music would wrap itself around her with force and vigor and vim and verve.

She sat down.

The music transported her. It was one of the records she had half-heard the night before when Bobby had taken her in her strong arms and had shown her the beauties of the world. And now, with the same record playing, every act and every emotion and every sensation of the previous night returned to haunt her.

She could not sit still. The music was powerful, beautiful, majestic. But, much as she wanted to hear it, she could not sit still.

Finally she gave up. She rose from the chair, walked to the

stereo set, flicked the reject lever again and stood still while the tone arm rose again, retreated from the record, and lowered itself to bed. Then there was a sharp click and the stereo was still. She took off the record, holding it by the edges so as to avoid damaging the grooves, and returned it to its jacket. She put the record back where it belonged and left the living room.

When she came to the closed door of Dave's den she knocked once, firmly. For a moment she heard nothing. Then his voice, asking what she wanted.

"I have to go out for a few minutes," she said. "You don't mind, do you?"

"Where to?"

"We're out of coffee," she said. "And cigarettes. And I promised Judy Garelnick I'd drop by with that chafing dish of mine she needs for her party. And—"

"God," he said. "And I thought I led a busy life. Go ahead. Take your time."

"I'll be back as soon as I can."

"Right."

She hurried then, snatching up her purse, grabbing a jacket from the closet, scurrying out the door. The car was in the garage where she had left it the night before. She fitted her key into the ignition slot, turned it, shifted into reverse and stepped down on the gas pedal. She backed out of the driveway to the street and began to drive.

Soon she was parking the car. Then she was walking, and then she was standing in front of a door, and then at last she was ringing a bell and then, then the door was opening.

"Come in."

She looked at Bobby, letting her hot eyes roam over Bobby's body, wanting to put her hands where her eyes were looking.

"You didn't call," Bobby said. "And I didn't dare call you. I suppose I could have. A husband doesn't get suspicious when another *woman* calls his wife. But I didn't. Come on inside. Take a chair. I've got a pot of coffee on the stove. You'll have a cup, won't you? I make good coffee."

"I know you do," Nancy said.

"Then I'll pour you a cup. Just a minute, I'll take care of it, I—"

Nancy was standing up now. "Don't," she said. "Don't bother. I don't want any coffee."

"Are you sure?"

"Positive."

"Food, then," Bobby said. "You'll have something, won't you? Will you let me give you something to eat?"

Nancy giggled. "Something to eat," she said. "That's it. You hit the nail right on the head. Give me something to eat, will you, Bobby? I'd like that. I really would."

Lucy had guessed at once that the man was poised, experienced, and sophisticated. A look at his clothing had indicated that he was not in danger of abject poverty.

But she had never imagined that he was anywhere near as rich as he was. Never before had she taken a ride in a Mercedes-Benz 300SL. Never before had she wound up in the East Sixties, and never before had a butler opened a door for her. When she realized that Jeff lived, not in an apartment but in the entire house she was probably taken aback. She had accepted as fact the idea that nobody in Manhattan lived in a private home. All Manhattan people lived in apartments. She was sure of this.

But Jeff had the whole house to himself. And it was more than a house.

It was a mansion.

Hand-hewn oak beams lined the twelve-foot ceilings. Oak paneling, old and magnificent, covered the walls. The carpet was deep and wine-red. She recognized a few of the paintings on the walls as ones she had seen in her high school art appreciation course, and she knew at once that they were originals, not copies.

"I'm rich," Jeff said, simply.

"I sort of thought so."

"Very rich. I could show you the whole house and you could marvel at the splendor of it, but it would be a waste of time for both of us. We're not interested in interior decoration, are we? Unless it's the decoration of your interior, which is another matter entirely."

She wasn't exactly sure what he was talking about. But it sounded nice.

"Come with me," Jeff said. "There's one room in particular that I want you to see. It's a special room for special events. You are a special event."

She followed him up a winding staircase to a room with a massive oak door. From his pants pocket he brought forth a small brass key. He unlocked the door and led her inside. Then he reached to turn on a light and the room was bathed in a soft red glow. There did not seem to be any lights. The light came from half a hundred neon bulbs buried in the four walls and ceiling.

Her first thought was that she was walking on the softest and deepest carpet ever invented. Then she realized her mistake. The floor was not carpeted at all. What seemed to be a carpet was actually a single mattress that covered the entire floor of the room. In a sense, the room was the largest bed in the history of the western world.

"A virgin," Jeff said reverently. "Well, virgin, here is the place where you will change your status. I think you know the rules. I call the shots. You do everything that I tell you to do."

She nodded dumbly.

Jeff smiled. "Let me explain the procedure to you," he said. "First you are going to undress for me. Slowly, in accordance with my instructions. Then you are going to remove my clothes as well. Do you understand?"

"Yes."

"Then you will sit down," he went on. "On the floor. I will sit down beside you. Before I sit down, however, I will throw a switch. This will start the projector. "

"Projector?"

He nodded. "Projector. We are going to watch a movie. Before we do anything else, we are going to watch a movie. I want you to pay close attention to it. It's a rather special sort of movie of a kind you're probably unacquainted with. Watch carefully. It will probably be instructive."

She had an idea what he meant. And she felt herself getting excited. She had never seen a movie like that before, although she had heard about them. Some of the boys in her class had gone to a fraternity convention in Passaic and a movie had been shown there. A vulgar movie. She wondered what it would be like, watching a movie with men and women doing things in it. Her heart was beginning to pound.

"During the movie," he continued, "I will caress you. You will probably feel yourself growing excited. You will want to kiss me, to respond to me. But I do not want you to do this. I want you to keep your eyes on the screen, to do nothing until the movie is over. Do you understand?"

"I understand."

"When the movie ends, it will be another matter entirely. Then I will make a woman out of you in the full sense of the word. I will teach you as much about sex as you will ever need to know in this world or the next. But in the meantime, remember what I have said. Do not touch me, do not look away from the screen, do not respond."

"Can I ask you a question?"

He seemed surprised. "What?"

"Why can't I . . . respond?"

He laughed a patronizing laugh. "Silly little virgin," he said. "The greater the anticipation, the better the act itself. The more intense the build-up, the more profound and far-reaching the ensuing passion. The longer you wait the better it will be. Understand?"

She nodded.

"Then we can begin," he said. "You may undress now. Take your time."

She felt very self-conscious. But she knew that she was going to experience a tremendous amount of sheer physical pleasure in the next few hours and she was excited. So she stood before him and took a deep breath.

First she took off her shoes, then her socks. Then her hands fastened on the waist of her sweater and drew it slowly, tantalizingly over her head.

Next the bra. It was hard for her to get the bra unclasped. Her fingers refused to behave. But at last she managed to get the hook open and the bra fell away from her breasts. She felt the warmth of his gaze upon her, and the warmth communicated itself very strongly to her. She began to breathe more heavily.

She opened her skirt, stepped out of it. She was wearing a half-slip and she took her time drawing the sheer silk down over her hips and off. Her panties were black—she had had to screw up her courage before she had the nerve to ask the salesgirl for them—but now she was glad she had bought them after all. The way he was staring at them, his eyes blazing, convinced her that they were appropriate.

She took off her panties.

He smiled. "Lovely," he said. "Now turn around. I want a good look at you."

She turned around.

"Lovely. All right, turn around again. Now come here and undress me."

She undressed him somewhat more quickly than she had undressed herself. She was careful with his clothing, realizing that it was very expensive. She took off each piece of clothing in turn, folding it carefully and placing it on the floor a ways away.

She had trouble repressing a desire to throw her arms around him and cover him with steaming kisses.

"Now sit down."

She sat down. He walked away for a moment and she heard

a click as he threw the switch. The lights—the red glow—went dim. And the projector began to whirr softly. She heard his footsteps as he approached her again. Then he sat down beside her. Together they stared at the screen, a white section on the wall ahead of them.

She watched the screen in total fascination.

TITLE CARD: BEDROOM FROLICS.

Despite the title, the first shot is of the interior of a bathroom. The camera opens, poetically, with a close-up of a bathtub. There is a woman in the tub. She is showering, rubbing soap over herself and letting the spray of water pelt down upon her.

The camera studies the woman. She is about medium height, with plain brown hair a little shorter than shoulder length. Her figure is on the overblown side. Her breasts are very large, jutting out firmly with no sag.

The girl lathers her breasts and the camera dollies in for a close-up. Then the girl lets the soap glide downward and the camera pans to follow the movements of the soap. The girl moves her thighs and begins to soap herself thoroughly in that area. The camera investigates meticulously.

The girl steps out of the shower, turns off the water, and dries off with a large towel, rubbing herself briskly. Then, majestically, she sits down on the edge of the tub and stretches. The camera again studies very closely the various aspects of the situation.

The girl pantomimes a sigh. She takes her breasts in her hands and gives them a good squeeze.

SUBTITLE: "THAT'S JUST WHAT I NEEDED. NOW WHAT I WANT IS A MAN."

The girl gets up and walks out of the bathroom. Now, in accordance with the title of the film, she is in a bedroom. It is furnished simply and cheaply—a dresser, a pair of cane-bottom chairs, a double bed, a night table. The girl hurries over to the bed and lies down on her back. The camera observes this dispassionately.

Shot of the door.

SUBTITLE: "IF YOU'RE A MAN, COME ON INSIDE!"

The door opens. The visitor, of course, is a man. He is a tall, heavyset with a thick black beard. He wears dungarees and a sweatshirt. The camera shows his face contorted in an expression combining surprise at the discovery of the girl and excitement at her appearance.

SUBTITLE: "WASH YOUR WINDOWS?"

Shot of the woman's face, smiling.

SUBTITLE: "COME HERE."

Shot of the man's face, smiling.

He undresses and the camera studies him while he does so. Then he comes over to the bed.

The man smiles. He touches her and she grins hysterically. He probes with the finger and she writhes in pleasure.

Shot of woman's face.

SUBTITLE: "YOU'VE GOT SOMETHING BETTER TO DO. NOW HURRY UP!"

The man does as he is told. He settles himself with her and they begin. The camera thoughtfully examines their activity.

They were not on the couch now. They were in Bobby's bed, together. And Nancy was deliriously happy.

"I want to do it with you," she said. "And I want you to do it with me. I want both and I can't decide which I want more and we better do one or the other before I go out of my mind. I can't take it, Bobby."

The brunette smiled. She leaned over, kissed Nancy on the mouth.

"We can do both, darling."

"Huh?"

Bobby laughed. "Your hall advisor wasn't much for advice," she said. "You don't know a hell of a lot, do you?"

"I don't get it."

"You can with me," Bobby said, "and I can with you."

"How?"

Bobby explained.

Graphically.

"Oh," Nancy said.

"Are you ready?"

"I guess so."

"Then let's get started."

"Okay."

They stretched out on the bed.

They were head-over-heels in love.

The brown-haired girl with the large breasts and the man had made love many times in many ways. Now they were lying together on the bed on their backs.

Shot of the door.

SUBTITLE: "COME ON IN IF YOU'RE A MAN!"

The door opens and another man comes in. He has curly hair and he is wearing dungarees and a sweatshirt.

Subtitle: "Wash your windows?"

Shot of the man's face now as he takes in the couple on the bed. His expression is the same combination of surprise as was seen before when the first man entered the room and saw the girl on the bed.

Shot of girl's face.

Subtitle: "I can handle both of you."

The man undresses and approaches the two of them. The girl smiles; she seems ready for anything.

Subtitle: "Let's find a new way."

They find a new way.

The camera watches dispassionately.

When they have finished, the two men switch places and the game begins again.

Eventually they finish this activity. The three of them sit together on the edge of the bed, the girl in the middle.

Subtitle: "That was fun!"

Shot of the three, their faces wreathed in smiles.

Subtitle: "More fun than washing windows."

Shot of the windows, for some strange reason.

Subtitle: "This was a real bedroom frolic."

Title card: THE END

Jeff's voice when he spoke was pitched low. He seemed to be completely in control of himself and Lucy could not understand how he managed it.

Because she was not in control of herself. As a matter of fact, she had a great deal of trouble accepting the fact that she had managed to sit through the movie without screaming her young lungs out. The movie had been the most erotic thing she had ever imagined, and she would have been highly aroused seeing it all by herself. Jeff's presence added to the excitement, and Jeff's activity multiplied it by an infinite amount.

"Well," he was saying, "did you find the film interesting?"

"It was . . . exciting."

"I see," he said. "And now are you ready?"

She nodded, breathless.

"Lie down."

She stretched out on her back. She closed her eyes and her head reeled.

"Don't move," he said.

Then he began.

The first thing she was conscious of was the most overwhelming pain she had ever felt in her life. The pain welled up within her and a shrill shriek tore forth from her lungs.

The pain went on.

And on.

And on.

She lay very still, and she wished that she had not come, that he was not doing this to her. She had waited for it, yearned for it, and now it was not good at all. There was no pleasure, nothing for her but pain.

And then something happened.

Something very strange.

Slowly the pain left. It was still there, a subtle undercurrent that never vanished entirely. But before it had been everything, and now that was no longer the case. It was present, but it was lower in intensity and it was being replaced a little at a time with something very different.

Something better.

Pleasure.

A warm feeling that spread through her whole body. A warm, tingling sensation that began to take possession of her, to excite her more than she had ever imagined she could be excited. At first she lay there inert, absorbing the thrills that coursed through her. But soon she discovered that it was becoming quite impossible to remain motionless. Her body had a will of its own.

She had, in the past, thought a great deal about making love. She had quite literally ached for it, and she had needed it so much that she was driven to the point of going out from bar to bar looking for a man who would initiate her into the mysteries. But even in her wildest dreams, in her most incredible fantasies, she had been unable to imagine anything like this. The petting she had done with boys like Joe Turley was an inadequate preparation.

The reading, the thinking—these had given her clues, but the reality so greatly over-shadowed such vicarious activities that she could not believe what was happening to her. She only knew that she wanted it to go on forever; to keep up eternally.

And, amazingly, it got better. It got increasingly better, pitching her even higher, until she thought that she was a bomb about to explode, a rocket ready to soar into the stratosphere and through it to the moon. Her body was sailing and her head was spinning so greatly that she was absolutely dizzy.

And then it began to happen. She knew what was happening. She had reached fulfillment before, reached it by coaxing herself.

But this was very different.

This was not furtive, self-induced and self-enjoyed. This was nothing of the sort.

And her brain spun madly as it happened, happened, happened for her, as she reached the very crest of an unstoppable wave, as the sun dimmed out and the moon went black. It happened and, simultaneously, it happened for him as well. They were locked in mortal combat and sensual love and the earth rocked by, coming slowly to rest, filling her with a peace unlike anything she had ever known.

She was limp, unable to move. Her eyes were shut because she did not have the strength to open them. Her arms were too heavy to be raised up. Her breathing was slowly, very slowly, returning once more to normal. Her heartbeat was still fast but it was slowing down again.

"You were very good, Lucy."

She couldn't even answer.

"Very good," he repeated. "I hurt you, didn't I? Hurt you badly."

"It's . . . all right."

He laughed. "I'm not apologizing," he said. "I meant to hurt you. It was very interesting, the way you began in extreme pain and shifted bit by bit from pain to pleasure. Very interesting. I enjoyed it."

"So did I."

"I noticed that," he said wryly. "And you really were a virgin, weren't you? I thought you were, but the only way to tell was to find out for myself. I've had virgins often enough before, but I doubt that I've ever had one quite like you. How old are you, Lucy?"

She told him.

"Excellent," he said, clapping his hands and grinning boyishly. "Seduction of a virgin and statutory rape combined! A wonderful way to spend an evening. Now have you any idea what's next on the agenda?"

She took a deep breath. She knew only that it was getting late, that she had better be heading home shortly. The night was a success and she was a virgin no longer. The next step was to head for home. Maybe he would be willing to drive her to Penn Station, or at least to call a cab for her.

"I'd better get home," she said.

"Are you kidding?"

She stared at him.

"You'll go home when I tell you to go home," he said. "Not

before. I'm not finished with you yet, not by a long shot. There are other things I must teach you first."

"But—"

"No buts," he snapped. "You've got your part of the bargain to carry off. You know the rules. You accepted them before we began. I make the rules. I call the shots. And you do what I tell you to do."

She opened her mouth to speak, then closed it without saying anything. He was right, of course. She had agreed to do what he asked her to do. She had not counted on more than once. Once, she thought, ought to be enough. Enough for anybody.

Then she remembered the movie. That was different, she told herself. They had to make the movie a long one, and as a result they did it over and over again. But normal people didn't.

Or did they?

"This is your first night," Jeff was saying. "It is the first time you and I have ever been together and it will very likely be the last. I rarely see the same girl more than once. You are very charming, but I still doubt that it will be desirable for us to get together again."

She wasn't unhappy about that. Jeff was good and she was glad she had met him and that he had been the first for her. But at the same time she was clever enough to see that there was something distinctly unhealthy about him. She knew that continued exposure to someone like him would be bad for her.

"So we are going to do everything," he said, emphasizing the final word of the sentence. "Everything there is to do. It is our only chance together and we are going to make the most of it. You might as well get that into your head."

She nodded, afraid to say anything.

"And now," he said, "we might as well get started. The next step in your education. This is one in which you'll have to take the initiative."

She wasn't sure what he meant.

"Remember the movie?"

"Of course."

"Remember when the second man came into the room?"

She nodded.

"Remember the girl and the second man?"

"Oh," she said.

"You're going to do that to me."

"No—"

"No? Oh, but you are. You are going to do what she did and more. You are going to do a good job."

"No," she said, her stomach churning. "It's not natural. It's vulgar. I won't do it."

"You won't?"

She shook her head.

"If you don't," he said menacingly, "I'll make you regret it. Do you know what I'll do to you?"

She stared at him.

"I won't kill you," he said. "But I'll make you wish that I had. When I finish with you no man will ever so much as look at you again. Your face will look as though it had been stepped on. Your breasts will be two hunks of raw meat. Your legs will be broken."

She gasped. He wouldn't do anything like that to her. No man would.

Then she looked at him, sensing the monumental evil within

him. And she knew instinctively that he would do just what he threatened to do.

"No," she said.

He said nothing.

"You wouldn't."

He still remained silent.

"You would," she said. "You really would."

He nodded.

"All right," she said woodenly. "Tell me what you want me to do. I'll do it."

He told her. Then he lay down on his back and closed his eyes. For a second or two she remained inert, unable to move. She was sick to her stomach, sick at what she had to do. But she had no choice.

She had to begin.

And she began.

Her stomach was a knot ready to turn itself inside-out, ready to empty itself of its contents. She felt that she couldn't go on another minute, that it was too much for her, that she would rather take the punishment than go on with her task. He could beat her and disfigure her and it would not be nearly so bad as what he was forcing her to do. Nothing could be this bad. Nothing in the world could make her so unhappy, so wretched, so sick, so miserable.

But she went on.

Grimly she tried to disassociate herself from what she was doing. She tried to let her mind concentrate on some other thing, some alien topic. She tried counting: one, two, three, four, five, six, seven, eight, nine, ten, eleven—

It was no use.

His passion was a living thing now, flowing with pleasure, and she knew what was going to happen. She knew it, and this only made everything a thousand times worse, a thousand times more horrible. She didn't want it to happen because it would be so disgusting, and at the same time she did want it to happen because then it would be over, over forever, over once and for all ...

He was still lying on his back on the floor when she was already fully dressed. She dressed slowly, amazing herself with the methodical nature of her own movements. It was as though she was no longer a person at all, no longer either girl or woman, but a mindless and brainless robot instead. She functioned automatically, her mind somewhere else.

She put on her panties. They did not look exciting any more. Now they were dirty. Everything was dirty, tasteless, vile, disgusting.

She put on her bra. She wanted to cut off her breasts, to get rid of everything about her that was sexual. Sex was vile, terrible, rotten.

She put on her sweater, her skirt. She put on her socks and her shoes. She tied her shoes and stood up.

His eyes opened.

"Where are you going?"

"Home."

He laughed. "Tired already? Bored with the fun and games? Ready to leave?"

"I hate you," she said.

"Do you?"

She said nothing.

"You shouldn't," he said. "You have no reason to. I gather that you didn't enjoy what I made you do."

"I hated it."

"Your privilege," he told her. "But you made a bargain. You shouldn't hate me for holding you to it."

"That's not why I hate you."

"Why, then?"

"Because you're disgusting."

"And you're a fool."

She stared hard at him. She was a fool? Because she was not as disgustingly twisted as he was? That didn't make her a fool. It made her a human being and it made him an animal. That was all there was to it.

"A fool," he repeated. "Anyone who thinks another person is disgusting because of that person's sexual desires is a fool. Worse than a fool. An idiot."

He sat up. "Look at it this way," he said. "You may not like some of the things that I like. That's your privilege, as I said. But to say that I'm disgusting because of what I like is outlandish and illogical. Suppose another girl detests sex in any form. Is it right for her to think of you as disgusting?"

She thought about that one. A lot of girls, she knew, would think so. A lot of girls never even petted and had nothing but contempt for girls who went all the way. Was *she* disgusting, then? She didn't think so. She had desires and she gave in to them. But by that line of reasoning . . .

"You see? You may think I enjoy things you would not enjoy. I suspect you'd enjoy them yourself in time, but I won't argue about that point. If you can think I'm disgusting, I can think you're a lifeless prude. I don't. I think you have a right to be whatever you are. I'm more generous in that respect than you are."

"But—"

"Relax," he said. "You'll never see me again. You'll never have to do anything with me again. So relax. I enjoyed this evening, and I know damned well that you enjoyed it too. You don't think so now, but later you'll remember how much fun you had and you'll forget how much you hated the second item on the menu. I guess *menu* really applies, doesn't it? But forget it, as I said. You'll treasure tonight. It'll light up your life. So relax and be happy."

She didn't say anything.

"You want to go home now. huh?"

"That's right."

"Hang on," he said. "I'll give you a ride."

"Don't bother."

"It's not that much trouble," he said. "I like to drive. I have a good car and it's a pleasure. Especially at night when the roads are clear."

"I'd rather take the train."

"Why? Do you hate me that much?"

She didn't answer.

"It won't kill you to ride in the same car with me," he said. "I won't even try to kiss you goodnight. And it will get you home one hell of a lot faster. You don't want to get in very late, do you?"

"No."

"Then take the ride. Get down off your high horse and

remember that you're every bit as human as I am. You're nothing special. You're a person, too."

She took a deep breath.

"Sit down," he said. "The Mercedes even has bucket seats. You'll have a seat all to yourself. And with the top down you can breathe nice fresh air. You won't even have to inhale the odor of me. What more can you ask for?"

She thought about it and had to admit to herself that he was right. Maybe he was right about everything—she did not know. But he was definitely right that she ought to accept a ride home with him. It wouldn't hurt her. And it would get her home much more speedily than the Long Island Railroad, which would take several hours.

"All right," she said.

"Have a seat," he said. "I'll get dressed. And then you can go back to your own sterile little bed and sleep."

She sat down, feeling a little bit ridiculous, while he put on his clothes. Then he filled his pipe again, lit it, and took her arm.

They left the room, and the house.

He drove fast. The wind whistled through her hair and the stars twinkled overhead. She sat in her own bucket seat and stared out into the night, wishing he would get her home. She was anxious to get home. She was anxious, for one thing, to take a long shower and wash the memory of him from her body.

She remembered the girl in the movie. Taking a shower. Making love.

They went over the bridge from Manhattan to Queens. Then something occurred to her and her heart missed a beat.

"Jeff—"

"What's the matter?"

"I just thought of something."

He sighed. "Something important, no doubt. Something earth-shaking and vital."

"Yes."

"Well, what is it?"

"You didn't use anything."

"Huh?"

"So I wouldn't get pregnant. You know."

He laughed.

"You didn't," she said accusingly. "And now I'll get pregnant. I'll get pregnant!"

His laughter sang in her ears and she wanted to kill him. But then he stopped laughing and told her she had nothing in the world to worry about.

"What do you mean?"

"Simple," he said. "I'm sterile."

"I don't believe it."

"I don't give a damn whether you believe it or not. I'm sterile. I've got a doctor's certificate to prove it. It comes in handy when broads like you spring a paternity suit. The suit never gets to court, somehow."

"But—"

"I had a disease once," he said.

"A disease?"

"A disease. Don't look at me like that, for Christ's sake. You're not infected. It's something I had about ten years ago and I don't have it any more. But it sterilized me. I can't possibly father a child."

"Honestly?"

"Honestly. So don't worry about a thing, sweetheart. All is well. You're not knocked up."

They rode the rest of the way in silence. At her insistence he let her off a few doors from her house and she walked home by herself. His car sped away noisily into the night and she looked after him, not knowing whether or not to hate him. At least, she thought, the evening had accomplished what it was supposed to. She was a virgin no longer. She was experienced.

And there was more. She had found out, amazingly enough, that she enjoyed it. Enjoyed it? She loved it. Making love with a man was easily the greatest thing ever.

Even the hideous thing he had made her do could not erase the memory of what had gone before. And what had gone before had been simply divine. The mere memory of it made her tingle from head to toe.

She unlocked the door with her key. All the lights in the house were out. Her parents were either asleep or faking it magnificently. She tiptoed upstairs and went into her own bedroom.

She was tired and she wanted to sleep. But she couldn't go to sleep at once.

Other things came first.

She showered for twenty minutes. She scrubbed herself until her skin glowed.

That was not all.

After she had showered she took toothbrush in hand and used plenty of toothpaste.

She brushed her teeth fifteen times.

CHAPTER 8

If all people were the same, life on this planet would be an intolerable bore. But all people are not the same. People are very different, as a matter of fact, and the variety of classmates, not in boys her own age, but in older men, she has become very much the individual rather than the faceless cipher.

Thus we have three individuals living secret lives, all of them on the same block in the same suburban community, two of them in one house and the third around the corner.

Obviously something must happen to them. For the past week their desires have been taking shape, crystallizing, developing. Their lives have been growing exceedingly complex. Something, inevitably, has got to give.

This is especially true in light of the dilemma each in turn is faced with. Nancy Grantland needs the pleasures and joys of lesbian love. Yet she is limited in her pursuit of these pleasures and joys by the outward role she is forced to play. She is still the suburban housewife on the surface.

Thus she has problems.

So does Dave Grantland. He needs young girls just as Nancy needs women. And his need, like hers, is just that. It is not simply a lust, but a genuine physical and emotional need. Without the release and pleasure he can receive only with young girls he cannot possibly be happy.

But the only outlet open to him is that afforded to him by professional child-prostitutes. The financial burden of such contacts would be too much for him to bear up under, and the physical pleasure involved is inevitably tempered by the fact that such contacts are, at root, cold and emotionless, sterile and unproductive. Thus he, too, is frustrated.

And Lucy King is in much the same boat. She can, of course, continue to make visits to Manhattan, can continue to pick up men in bars and sleep with them. But, as with Nancy and Dave Grantland, she will constantly be haunted by fear of discovery and consequent public and private shame. And her contacts with men will be one-sided, necessarily brief, necessarily guilt-ridden.

Three individuals.

Three troubled souls.

Three people with three problems.

Where are three solutions?

It was Wednesday. Dave Grantland sat alone at his desk. The copy for the Krutchmeir-Philbert account swam before his eyes. He had to grind out a twenty-second television spot for the account. A twenty-second spot lasts, generally, eighteen seconds. At a normal human speech rate of one hundred twenty words per minute, an announcement running eighteen seconds would consist of thirty-six words. Since announcers reading spots can read somewhat faster than the norm, the general length of a "twenty-second spot" is in the neighborhood of fifty words.

Fifty words on the merits of Krutchmeir-Philbert products was no simple matter. With so little room to move around in, Dave had to make every word do the work of three or four. The spot had to be loaded with the right words, the words that motivation-research had predicted would carry the proper weight, sneak in with the proper Freudian message, and otherwise mesmerize the viewers as thoroughly as possible in the eighteen available seconds.

Dave had been sitting at his desk for three hours. In that time he had already managed to knock out a ten-second spot for the same account. Ten second spots, with only twenty or twenty-five words open, were paradoxically easier. There the copywriter had so little room that he couldn't go wrong. Everything was structured; the copywriter just had to set down the slogan of the week and let it carry the ball.

But the twenty-second spot had been bugging him consistently for the bulk of the preceding three hours. It wouldn't go right. Worse, he couldn't keep his mind on it. Now he ground out a cigarette in the large and slightly futuristic ashtray that sat on his desk and looked down at the pencil in his other hand.

He had been doodling. He looked at the doodles now and shuddered involuntarily. On the top sheet of the small pad of unlined yellow paper he had drawn a girl. He had drawn her crudely but photographically. The little drawing would have been more appropriately placed on the wall of a men's room than on Dave Grantland's desk.

The drawing was, inevitably, of a young girl. She was not wearing any clothes in the sketch. She lay, stark naked, upon a small vaguely defined bed. Her head was tossed back, her breasts rampant.

The most striking thing in the sketch, more provocative even than the meticulous care used to make the girl lifelike, was the expression on her face. It was a child's face, and at the same time it was the face of a wanton—alive with passion, inflamed with a lust that was evil, abandoned.

Dave stared. Then he tore the piece of paper from the pad and ripped it into a dozen small pieces. He checked the pad and discovered that the impression of the drawing had carried through to the next several sheets of paper. He tore each off in turn, ripped them into bits and deposited them in the ashtray.

For a second he was seized by an irresistible urge to touch a match to the pieces of paper in the ashtray. But he realized how melodramatic that would be, how absurd. He pictured the rest of the office regarding him with amusement while scraps of paper burned themselves to oblivion in his slightly-futuristic ashtray. He shuddered again—a more controlled shudder this time—and he emptied the ashtray into the leather-covered trapezoid wastebasket beneath his desk.

Another cigarette sprang forth from the pack on his desk, found its way to his lips. A match burst into flame and the tip of his cigarette glowed with life. His lungs filled to overflowing with magnificent clouds of smoke. He held the smoke in, then let it trail forth from slightly parted lips. He smoked thoughtfully, remembering.

The night before—Tuesday night—he had gone to Hassan's. Once again he called Nancy at the shop where she worked, once again he told her that he would have to work late, that she should expect him when she saw him. She was trusting, sympathetic, and did not seem overly distressed at the prospect of being alone for the evening. It made him feel just that much worse, knowing that he was fooling her, that he was quite successfully stealing time for his aberration from her. He almost wished she would suspect him, put detectives on his trail, find him out. Her lack of knowledge only multiplied his own stabbing feelings of guilt.

But, that night, he once more ate dinner out. He went to an Armenian restaurant in Greenwich Village and ate a plate of mushroom kebab with wild rice. He had a few glasses of good red wine with dinner and followed it up with a cup of thick Armenian coffee. The coffee was very strong, the food delicious.

Then he had gone to Hassan's. Once more he sat while the waiter brought him coffee. This time he ordered a plate of baklava with his coffee and ate the sweet honey-and-walnut pastry while he waited for Kyros to appear. Once more Kyros came, and this time there was even less verbal fencing than before.

Nephrida was unavailable. But another girl could be seen, a girl the same age as Nephrida. And the price was only fifty dollars, twenty dollars less than Nephrida had cost him.

But the evening had been a disappointment. He sighed softly, remembering it. Nephrida had led him to expect far more from a professional prostitute than he had had any right to expect. The new girl—a young Irish girl named Moira—had been almost as pretty and every bit as adept at her business. But the fact that the affair was a business transaction and nothing more was a fact the girl made no attempt to hide. The appalling sterility, the coldness—these things were bad, very bad. They took the joy out of the affair and left only sex.

Sex. And on that score Dave was more than annoyed. Despite the artificiality of it all, despite the coldness and crassness and downright commercialism, the sex had been necessary and discomfortingly enjoyable. He had needed the sexual part of the evening and it had been enough in its own way to compensate for all that was lacking. More than enough.

He ground out his cigarette—savagely, this time. The only thing that the girl Moira had been able to offer was her youth. And that made the difference. She was cold and distant and totally impersonal.

But she was young, and that was somehow all that seemed to matter in the final analysis.

He cursed her and himself. He resolved to avoid Hassan's, to turn monastic if need be. And he wondered just how long he would be able to keep that vow, just how long he would be able to stay away from the promise of girlish love.

He cursed himself again, cursed himself for a fool and an abnormal and an idiot. Then he picked up his pencil and pushed the pad of unlined yellow paper in front of him. Rapidly and purposefully he began blocking out the copy for the twenty-second Krutchmeir-Philbert account.

"It can't go on like this, Nance!"

The voice belonged to Bobby. They were alone in the shop. A teenager had entered during the high school's lunch hour to buy a generously padded bra. Since then the store had been empty except for the two of them. They had maintained something approaching silence toward one another. Now Bobby had broken the silence and Nancy felt her hands beginning to shake. The shaking was not a voluntary act on her part. It happened almost before she knew it, before she knew just why she was shaking. Then the full impact of Bobby's words sank in and the shaking got worse instead of getting better. She wanted to say something but she didn't know what it was that she wanted to say.

"This is bad, Nance. This living a lie. This hiding. This sharing you with your husband. Damn it, I don't want to share you. I want all of you or none of you. None of this in-between nonsense. None of this where you don't even call the shots—where we wait for your husband to work late and then run off for a fast hour for ourselves. That's no good, baby. It's not natural. I'd rather give you up than string along with you on that basis. It's rotten."

In a way she was glad Bobby had said it, had brought it out into the open. She herself felt about the same way. Last night, when she and Bobby had been together while Dave worked late at the office, the satisfaction she had grown to expect from their relationship had been tempered with something else. It was disquieting, alarming.

"You want the moon," Bobby said. "And so we go on hiding ourselves from the world. You ought to move out on him, Nance. You ought to give him the air once and for all. You don't have any kids to worry about. It's not as though you're breaking up a home by getting a divorce. You're just ending a marriage that didn't have any right to exist from the beginning. You think you're being fair to him this way? You think it's fair to sneak out on him and carry on behind his back?"

She hung her head.

"Believe me," Bobby went on, "you're not doing the guy any

favors. You're not giving him any great bargain, living with him and sleeping with me. And I'll tell you something else, Nance. Something pretty significant, the way I see it. You don't really give a damn whether you're hurting him or not. You think so but it's nothing but rationalization. Deep down inside yourself you're nothing but selfish."

The words stung. Nancy stared, wishing there was something she could say. She opened her mouth to deny the charge, then closed it without speaking at all.

"It's the truth," Bobby said. "The truth. You want to have all the kicks of what we give each other without any of the penalties. You're a lesbian from beginning to end and you don't want to admit it to yourself. You want a home and a husband so that it won't hurt you to look in the mirror. Honey, I've been looking in the mirror for a good long time now. I didn't like the reflection at first. But I got used to it. I'm a lesbian. I'm neither proud of it nor ashamed of it. I am what I am. That's all there is to it. I don't fight it and I don't repress it and I don't hide it by shacking up with a faggot. You find plenty of dykes who pull a bit like that. Marry a fairy and everybody plays his own games. Not me. I don't advertise but I don't build walls and hide behind them. And that, my sweet, is precisely what you're doing. You don't want the world pointing fingers at you so you stay married to Dave. That's no good, Nance. No good for you and no good for me."

"What am I supposed to do?"

"Get a divorce."

"I don't believe in divorce."

Bobby snorted. "I don't believe in marriage," she said. "So we're even. But you've got to make up your mind, kitten. You're the nicest thing I've gotten next to in a long time and I like having you around. Maybe I'm even in love with you, whatever the hell that means. But I'll be damned a dozen times before I'll share you with the rest of the world. You're mine all the way or you're not mine at all. You've got to make up your mind."

"Can I have a cigarette?"

Bobby gave her a cigarette. She leaned forward and accepted a light from the brunette, her head whirling. She drew in smoke and blew it out.

"You're not being entirely fair," she said. "You know that, don't you?"

"How do you mean?"

"Just what I said, that's what I mean. You're not being fair with me."

"How?"

Nancy took a breath. "I . . . slept with a girl while I was in college. Then I got married and for ten years the only person who ever as much as touched me was my husband. Then, less than a week ago, I met you. And we went to bed. Right?"

"Right."

"And now you want me to turn my whole life upside-down. No matter how I feel, it takes a little while for a girl to get used to the idea of something like this. I've been married for ten years, Bobby. Maybe the marriage Dave and I have isn't the best marriage in the world. I'll grant you that. But it's not the worst in the world either. We've both tried. We've both been through a lot together. Maybe you're right and maybe the only fair thing is for me to get a divorce. But it's not that simple. Even if I can accept a divorce intellectually, I have to get used to the idea on an emotional plane. I have to think about it and . . . and *feel* about it. You can't rush me. You can't push me to one decision or another because it's no good that way."

She broke off suddenly and looked away. Both of them were silent and the air in the shop seemed very thick, very thick. Finally Bobby spoke.

"Okay," she said heavily. "Maybe you're right."

Nancy didn't say anything.

"Maybe I push too hard. It's the type of person I am. And you've got to understand how hard it is for me to share you at all, Nance. It's rough. I want you all the time, not just when his royal highness happens to feel like putting in a little overtime at his Madison Avenue desk. So I've got a compromise for you, toots. Not an easy one. But the only one that will work."

"What is it?"

Bobby grinned softly. "You've got a week," she said. "A week to make up your mind. Fair enough?"

"Fair enough."

"During that week," Bobby went on, "you sleep alone. That is, you don't sleep with me. Not until you make up your mind. If you decide on a divorce it's you and me as long as we both want it that way. If it's no divorce, if you decide to stick with Desperate David, then it's no go. You quit your job and we get out of each other's lives."

"And we stay apart until I decide?"

"Uh-huh."

"But—"

"It's the only way," Bobby said. "Believe me, it's going to be tougher for me than it is for you. Damned tough. But it's the only way you'll make a decision. Otherwise we'll tumble in and out of bed and the situation won't change at all. It'll stay the same as it's been. Which is no good, toots. It has to be one way or the other. Not both."

"I guess you're right."

"Of course I am."

"It'll be hard all right. But we can work it out. And I think I know which way I'll decide, Bobby."

"On a divorce?"

"I think so," Nancy said. "Because I honestly don't think I could give you up. I need time to decide. But I can guess my decision."

"I hope so," Bobby said.

"So do I."

They touched hands once, briefly. Then the bell rang and Nancy went out to take care of a customer.

It was a bad Wednesday. Lucy King, who had just come home from school after having paid no attention whatsoever to what various teachers said in the course of the entire day, was lying on her bed with her eyes wide open. Her head was aching rather persistently and she knew that aspirin would not do her any good at all.

Lucy was unhappy. Unhappiness causes headaches quite often, and such headaches do not respond favorably to medication. So she lay on the bed and stared balefully at the ceiling and felt very miserable.

She had been with a boy the night before. A boy, not a man. And it had gone poorly.

She had been baby-sitting for Fred and Joanne Gavilan again. And once again she had had company. The company in this instance was not Joe Turley but a boy named Edgar Kalakinski. Edgar Kalakinski was renowned as the champion catman in Mataquois. By fair means or foul he had rolled up an impressive tally of female conquests. The means were generally fair. Once a boy had Edgar Kalakinski's reputation, girls went out with him knowing full well how the evening would end. As a result, each evening's battle was more than half won before it began. If a girl agreed to go out with Edgar Kalakinski, she had also agreed—silently—to sleep with him. Occasionally he dated a girl who did not know the score, but since he was a very dynamic young man who approached love as a bull fighter approached a bull, he rarely departed without a new scalp on his belt. He was good at seduction.

Lucy was well aware of Edgar Kalakinski's reputation. She also knew that he rarely discussed a conquest with the other boys. The word spread quite frequently, mainly because the girl herself was less adept at keeping a secret than was Edgar. But as far as Lucy knew, Edgar was the Sphinx in a Don Juan's body.

For this reason she surprised the daylights out of him by walking up to him at school and suggesting quite boldly that he help her baby-sit for the Gavilans that night.

Which was fine with Edgar.

Her reasoning was sound enough. Lucy wanted love. She wanted it very badly, and she wanted it with somebody who was properly experienced. She also wanted to avoid a repetition of Saturday night's experience. While Jeff Gardner had been a magnificent performer, he had also succeeded in making her feel filthy from head to toe.

Thus Lucy wanted experience and wanted to avoid the casualness of a bar pick-up. And thus she wound up with Edgar Kalakinski. But, like the best laid plans of mice and men, the best laid plans of Lucy ganged far aglay.

She had gone to the Gavilans' house at 7:15. The Gavilans had left five minutes later. And, ten minutes after the departure of Fred and Joanne Gavilan, Edgar Kalakinski had arrived at the house.

They began by watching television. Then, cleverly enough, Edgar let his arm steal around her shoulders. He kissed her, and she was happy to discover that he kissed very well. He kept on kissing her and she let herself respond to him.

Then, bit by beautiful bit, he had moved on to bigger and better things. First he toyed with her breasts, and then he ran his hand up her leg under her skirt, playfully but insistently.

Onward.

Ever onward.

Next came her blouse, then her bra, then her skirt, and her panties.

He had become a little awkward at that point. He had undressed himself, and in the meantime she lay there on the couch of the Gavilans waiting for him, wishing he would hurry. But he had taken an impossibly long time to get undressed, and then he had taken an even longer time donning armor. There was something disturbing about the whole idea. Lucy felt a little of her enthusiasm beginning to wane. But at last he was ready and he reached for her.

And it began.

It was hardly bad. She had wanted it, perhaps even more than she had thought she did.

And then it was over.

It was over much too quickly for her. Her heart began to beat wildly and her mouth went dry and her blood sang in her veins, and then suddenly he was gone and she was left alone to crawl the walls. She held him tight, wanting him to stay with her until it happened for her, wanting him to remain where he was until her passion had a chance to spill over around her and grant her fulfillment.

But that was not what happened.

He left her at once, drew away from her automatically while the passion was still growing within her. He had satisfied himself. That was all that mattered to him. The idea that he should stay with her until she was satisfied was quite obviously an idea that never entered his thick head.

She wanted to kill him. She wanted to pick up the heavy brass ashtray from the table beside the couch, and she wanted to pound away at his fat head with the ashtray until she succeeded in creating a large hole in his head. Then the sawdust could leak out, and to hell with him.

But she did not strike him. Instead she dressed in a hurry, turning away from him, and when she was dressed she turned and studied him.

"That was great," he said. "You know, you're okay. I never figured you'd be so good."

She said nothing because she had nothing to say to him. Not now and not ever.

And, hysterically, he was standing up. "Well," he was saying, "I guess I better go now. Got to go home and hit the books hard. Big test tomorrow. Advanced algebra. A real tough course, and the roughest part is that I need it for graduation. Better get home and get to work."

It was incredible. He had come over, had necked with her, had made poor love to her, and now, at once, he was leaving. He had put on his clothes and now was going to go home. She could hardly believe it.

"I'll walk you to the door," she said. She was trying to be sarcastic but the point was lost on him. He was not particularly subtle.

"Don't bother," he said. "You stay there. Rest up. I can find the door myself."

So she let him find the door himself. When he was gone she put the television set on again and tried to get lost in what was happening on the screen.

When she realized that she was crying she was amazed. She tried to laugh about it. The result was only that she went right on crying.

She cried for a long time. Then, resolutely, she sat up and dried her eyes. In the Gavilan bathroom she washed her face and combed her hair. Then she sat down once again in the living room and tried to relax.

Now, a day later, she was still trying to relax. She was having about as much success in the attempt as she had had the night before. It was not easy to relax. Not when you were Lucy King and you had Lucy King's problems. Then it was not a simple matter at all. It was pretty damned difficult, as a matter of fact. Well nigh impossible, when you came right down to it.

What it boiled down to was that she needed a man. The need for a man was no longer strictly a sexual need. She needed a man because, somehow, she had become far too mature for boys. Edgar Kalakinski had failed her on an emotional level even more than on a physical level. He knew how to make love. He was experienced. But he did not have any feeling for his partner. He was thoughtless and heartless and useless, as far as she was concerned, and neither he nor any boy like him could ever give her what she wanted so desperately.

Men were different. Even a man like Jeff Gardner, inconsiderate as he had been in so many respects, was far better for her than a boy like either Joe Turley or Edgar Kalakinski. A man could understand her. A man could make her feel like a woman instead of a girl. A man could fulfill her and make her happy.

She was not happy now. Not by any stretch of the imagination. On the contrary, she was wretched.

For the first time in her life, the years to come loomed in front of her like a gigantic prison. Her junior and senior years at high school, with more pointless dates and pointless classes and brainless companions. Four years of college, during which time she would date college boys and be romanced in an equally mindless manner. Then what? Marriage, no doubt, to someone her own age or a year or two older. And more of the same stupidity until finally she died.

A bright future.

A wonderful life ahead of her.

A monumental, pointless, senseless, pleasureless, miserable bore.

She tried not to cry and failed.

•   •   •

The inevitable meeting came the following night. Thursday night. In Mataquois.

Nancy Grantland, who was not part of the meeting, was in the kitchen. She was preparing dinner. For some obscure reason she had decided that dinner that night ought to be a real production. She was going to go out of her way to come up with a particularly good meal.

A potful of rice was cooking on the stove. A sauce was now developing in the electric frying pan. The sauce contained numerous spices, numerous mushrooms, and other goodies. The sauce was taking the form of an especially thick and especially good mushroom gravy.

In another frying pan on the stove large tender chunks of sirloin were browning, browning slowly in butter. When the meat was properly browned Nancy would put it in the fry pan with the sauce. She would simmer the result. Then she would prepare beds of fluffy rice on two plates, set the meat on the rice beds, and pour the mushroom sauce on top.

Another pot was filled with corn on the cob. A saucepan contained green peas. The meal was a production.

Outside, Dave Grantland was on his way home. He had just gotten off the Long Island train and was walking toward his house. He carried an attaché case in one hand, a copy of the *World-Telegram and Sun* under his other arm. He had put in a good day at the office and felt pleased with the fact.

When he turned the corner of Aberdeen Drive and headed toward his own house, Lucy King also turned the corner of

Aberdeen Drive a block away. Lucy, too, was on her way home. After school had ended for the day, she had gone over to Phyllis Langhorn's house to prepare the joint project they were to present before the English class. Phyllis was imaginative if not brilliant, and the planning session had gone well. Lucy had been surprised to discover that the project was going to be an interesting one. She glowed with a definite feeling of accomplishment.

The session with Phyllis had succeeded in taking her mind off a variety of problems about which she did not particularly want to think to begin with. And, as a result, she was quite happy.

They met three doors from Dave's house. Dave's first thought was that he had never seen this particular girl before. She did not look at all familiar at first and he wondered who she was and what she was doing there. He stopped dead in his tracks and looked at her. Then, suddenly, he recalled having seen her before and remembered at once who she was. She was Lucy King. She lived just around the corner.

"Oh," he said, feeling foolish. "It's you, Lucy. Didn't recognize you there for a minute."

And Lucy's first thought was that here in front of her was the most dramatically attractive man she had ever set eyes on. She, too, was at a loss for a moment. She did not recognize him any more than he recognized her. But when he spoke she remembered. He was Dave Grantland. He lived on Aberdeen, around the corner from her, and he had a very beautiful wife.

"Oh," she said. "Uh . . . hello, Mr. Grantland." It was strange. She had an almost irresistible impulse to call him not *Mr. Grantland* but *Dave*.

It was funny.

They stood there quite awkwardly for a very long moment. Then Dave remembered where he was and got ready to walk away. For some reason he couldn't just walk away, though. First he had to say something.

"Got to get home," he said. "Wife must have dinner ready by now. I'll see you, Lucy."

"Yes," she said, feeling strangely light-headed. "Yes, of course."

And she, too, turned to go home.

It's ridiculous, he told himself later, Nancy's good dinner in his stomach and a cigarette in his mouth.

Completely ridiculous. If I have a brain in my head, I'll stay away from that girl. God, that's just what I need. Something right in the neighborhood to play around with. They wouldn't put me in jail then. Not by a long shot. They'd kill me. Cut my throat and pound my face to a pulp. And it would be just what I'd deserve.

His heart was pounding.

She was so pretty. So damnably pretty. And there had been something in her eyes, unless he had imagined it, something that had said that she was just as interested in him as he was in her.

Ridiculous. He was imagining it. It was wishful thinking, pure and simple, and if he kept on thinking along those lines he was going to find himself in one hell of a mess. It was best to stop thinking. To forget. To ignore.

Forget that face? Ignore that body?

His hands shook and he dropped his cigarette. It rolled insanely along the carpet and he bent down, searching for it, afraid the rug would burn. He picked up the cigarette and drew on it. It tasted foul and he put it out.

Forget that face?

Ignore that body?

Trembling, he reached for another cigarette.

He wouldn't want you, Lucy King told herself. *He wouldn't want you in a million years.*

Or would he?

No, she thought sadly. He wouldn't. He had a beautiful wife, a lovely mature woman with a perfect face and a spectacular figure who would make Lucy look like a stick by comparison. He was happily married and he didn't look like the type to chase women.

And certainly not the type to chase girls.

I always want what I can't have, she thought. *It never fails. Never.*

He had seen her once, and she had seen him once, and now she wanted him. What in the world was the matter with her? He would never notice her, never pay the slightest bit of attention to her. As far as he was concerned she was a child.

But she wanted him.

God, how she wanted him!

She tried to forget him, tried to put her mind on her schoolwork. And failed.

Because she couldn't forget him. She was, incredibly, at the point of falling in love with him. Falling in love with a man more than twice her age, a happily married man who lived right around the corner from her.

And he would never be interested in her.

Not in a million years.

Chapter 9

How much of the meeting was by design and how much was a matter of coincidence is a question one cannot answer easily. In a sense it was entirely coincidental. In another sense it was purposeful on the part of both of them. Either interpretation seems equally valid.

On Dave Grantland's part, it must be said that he was careful to work until the same time Friday as he had on Thursday, that he took the same train home, and that he walked the same route from train to house. But also, one might add the fact that he usually worked until that time, that he'd often taken that train, and that he almost invariably walked home by that route, since it was the most direct course from station to home.

A similar chain of circumstances may be applied to Lucy King. After school she went once again to Phyllis Langham's house, where the two of them polished their presentation and worked diligently. She left Phyllis's house at precisely the same time she had left it the day before. It was a logical time to leave, and the hope of a meeting may or may not have been the main factor in her leaving at that time. Again, she took the same route home. It was the most direct route.

And they met.

This time the meeting was something noticed instantly and

consciously by both of them. This time each knew at once who the other was, and this time both felt acutely self-conscious immediately. And each read the face of the other for some sign, some clue, some indication that the enthusiasm was shared.

They stopped dead in their tracks.

They stared.

And they both began talking at once. Both mouths opened, both voices started—and stopped.

Then Dave said: "I can't believe it."

"Neither can I."

"But . . . it's true. For you, too. I can tell. I can honestly tell."

"Yes," she said.

He looked around. "We can't talk here," he said. "Not out in the open like this."

"Why not?"

"People will notice."

"They'll notice a man talking to a girl," she said, taking command of the situation. "They'll notice two neighbors meeting on the street. They'll never understand."

He nodded. She was right.

"I have to see you," he said. "Not on the street. Alone. In private."

"I know."

"We have to be together," he said. "We have to find out what's happening to us."

"I know."

"But where? How? When?"

She giggled softly. "You're all flustered," she said. "You don't have to be. Not with me. Remember, it's the same for me as it is for you."

He nodded. There was no need to pretend with her. Everything was very simple.

"Are you free tonight?"

"I can get away," she said. "I can meet you."

"Your parents—" He thought that her parents were not much older than he was. His face was flushed.

"I'll tell them I'm baby-sitting," she said.

"Can you get away with it?"

"Of course," she said. "I baby-sit a lot of the time. And my parents trust me."

"My . . . wife trusts me," he said slowly. "I can meet you. I guess."

"Where and when?"

He thought for a moment. "Eight o'clock," he suggested. "It that all right with you?"

"Of course."

"I'll take the car," he said, thinking on his feet. "I'll tell Nancy I'm playing poker with some fellows from work. I think she'll believe it."

She nodded.

"Where?"

She closed her eyes for a moment, trying to concentrate. "I'll walk to the corner of Hackney and Putnam," she said. "I'll get there about eight. You drive by and pick me up. I'll be waiting there for you."

"I won't be late."

"Neither will I."

He stood there for a moment, looking into her eyes, wanting to kiss her but not daring to do so. He compromised by taking her hand for a shadow of an instant. Then he released her and she drew away from him.

"I'll be there," he said. "Wait for me."

She nodded, quickly, unable to speak. Then they turned from each other and walked to their separate houses. They were both excited, heads swimming, knowing for certain that they were caught up together in something bigger than anything either of them had ever known before.

Nancy was trembling when she picked up the receiver. Her head ached dully and her eyes felt as though leaden weights were attached to the back of each eyeball. She cradled the receiver, then picked it up again and held it to her ear.

She dialed the number.

The phone rang three times. Then it was picked up at the other end and a woman's voice said: "Hello?"

"I have to see you," she said.

"I told you not to call me. Not until you've made up your mind one way or the other."

"I've made it up."

"And—"

"I'll get the divorce."

Bobby let out her breath. "I'm glad," she said. "I'm very glad. You've talked to him about it?"

"Uh . . . no."

"Why not?"

"I haven't had a chance," she said. "He's not home now. He went out to a poker game a minute ago. He won't be home until very late."

"You shouldn't have called me. You've made up your mind but you should discuss it with him before you call me."

Nancy gasped. "I have to see you, Bobby."

"I—"

"I have to see you. Can't you understand that? I'm all alone and I need you and I'm going out of my mind. I need you, damn it! And I have to see you and I've made up my mind and I'm not fooling you and—"

"Relax."

She tried to.

"You poor kid," Bobby was saying. "You're really going around in circles, aren't you?"

"Uh-huh."

"You're sure you aren't going to change your mind again, Nance? I don't want to play games any more."

"I'm positive, darling."

"I'm glad. I'm very glad. Well, in that case, I guess I shouldn't deny you the pleasures of my pure white body. You want to come over here?"

"He took the car."

"Well—"

"Bobby, why don't *you* come over *here*?"

"Is it safe?"

"Of course."

"He could come home early—"

"He said he'd be late. It's safe."

"All right," Bobby said. "I'll be right over."

She hung up. Nancy stood for several seconds holding the dead phone to her ear. Then, slowly, she replaced the receiver. She was so excited she could barely stand up.

Then she bustled around the house, putting everything in order, making the place as attractive as possible. She wanted Bobby to like her house. It was somehow very important.

She was pouring liquor over ice cubes when the bell rang. She carried the glasses in her hands as she walked to the door to admit the woman she loved.

"I can't believe it," Dave Grantland said. "I'm thirty-four. You must be around seventeen."

"I'm sixteen."

"God in heaven. Eighteen years difference. It's ridiculous, you know. Insane."

"But it happened."

"Yes," he said. "Yes. It happened."

They were sitting in the front seat of his Pontiac. He was driving aimlessly, barely aware of where he was going. He knew only that he was driving out of Mataquois. That much certainly made sense.

"Where do you want to go?"

"Anywhere," she said. "Anywhere at all. A hotel or a motel or the back seat of this car. It really doesn't matter where you make love to me."

He caught his breath. "Are you sure?"

"Positive."

"Think about it. Think what you're saying. Are you still sure?"

"I'm sure." She hesitated. "I'm not a virgin," she said. "I've done it before."

"That doesn't matter."

"I didn't think it would. But I wanted to tell you. And you'd better hurry. You'd better find a hotel or a motel or park somewhere before I come after you. I want you, Dave. It sounds funny—me calling you Dave. But it sounded even funnier yesterday when I called you Mr. Grantland. I felt ridiculous. Do you know what I mean?"

"I know."

She reached for him, touched his knee with one small hand. A bolt of electricity went through them both at once. She withdrew her hand as though it had been burned.

"A hotel," she said. "Or a motel. Hurry."

"I will."

He did not know where to look for a motel. But he let the car do the thinking and he drove until a neon sign flashed MOTEL on into the night, and he swung the wheel sharply and found a place to park.

The motel keeper, an aging balding man with a pot belly and an unpleasant expression, took ten dollars from Grantland and gave him a register to sign. Dave wrote *Mr. and Mrs. John Doe.* The motel keeper believed this not at all and could not have cared less.

The room was small and worth a good deal less than ten dollars a night. It was obvious that the motel existed to rent rooms to couples looking for a mating place. Ordinarily both Dave and Lucy would have found the atmosphere forced, unnatural and rather dirty. Now they did not mind at all. Something—they were not sure just what it was but could not doubt its existence—made the difference and transformed the squalid little room into a romantic haven.

There was a bed, sagging slightly in the middle and a little the worse for wear. There was a dresser, scarred irreparably by the butts of a million forgotten cigarettes. There was a sink in one corner, a wastebasket in another. The linoleum that covered part of the floor was worn and cracked. The picture on the wall was pretty terrible—a beagle pointing out a pheasant, a hunter taking aim, all done in extremely poor imitation of photographic realism.

But the room was divine.

"You can still change your mind," he told her, and she smiled back at him, letting him know that he was wrong, that she could not possibly change her mind, that she was personally committed to the end.

"So could you," she said. "You could get twenty years for this. That's a long time."

"I'll risk it."

"Will you?"

"Uh-huh."

He walked toward her, reached out his arms for her. She came to him with a little cry that tore itself free from deep within her throat. She buried her face in his chest and she felt the pressure of her breasts against his chest. He kissed her.

"You had a drink," she said.

"I needed one."

"Were you afraid of me?"

"Partly of you," he admitted. "More of myself. Afraid of the world, too."

"I'm not afraid."

"Neither am I," he said. "Not now."

They walked to the side of the bed like creatures in a dream. She sat down on the edge of the bed and he sat down beside her, his eyes drinking in the beauty of her, his hands itching for contact with her sweet cool flesh.

"Undress for me," she said. "I want to see you."

He stood up and began to undress, not feeling self-conscious at all. He remembered the time he had undressed in front of Nephrida and recalled how the young Egyptian girl had taken his clothing from him a piece at a time and had hung everything up in the tiny closet.

But the episode seemed to have happened a thousand years ago. This was entirely different. Completely different. This was between him and Lucy. And he loved her.

She watched him now. She saw how strong he was, saw the loose muscles in his arms and legs. He had hair on his chest and she was glad of that. She wondered how it would feel to have her bare breasts against his hairy chest. She decided that it would probably feel very nice.

She watched until he was naked. She decided that everything about him pleased her immensely. And her flesh grew warm at the sight of him.

"My turn," she said, simply. He sat down on the edge of the bed once more and she stood up, removing her clothing. She took off everything until she was naked just as he was.

Then she sat down again, loving the look of passion in his eyes, loving the way his eyes reflected her beauty. He kissed her and his tongue entered her mouth and she knew that everything was going to be all right now, that it would be good for her, better than she had ever imagined it could be. He kissed her again and she pressed against him and felt his hairy chest against her bare breasts and it felt good, very good, even better than she had expected.

Slowly, automatically, the two of them stretched out full length upon the bed. Dave's hands reached for the girl, touching her, caressing her. He let out a slight gasp of wonder at the perfection of her.

"You're so beautiful."

"As beautiful as she is?"

He stared at her questioningly.

"Your wife."

"Forget her," he said. "She's . . . a woman I've lived with for ten years. Nothing more. She doesn't matter."

She smiled and kissed him. He hadn't been prepared for such a show of passion on her part and he almost fell off the bed. But instead he grabbed her and what had begun as a kiss swiftly developed into something more.

He kissed her again and again, and she was ready.

The bed, veteran of a countless multitude of love battles, screeched in protest. The room seemed to dip and soar, intoxicated by the throbbing pungent rhythm, caught up in the force and fervor of lovemaking that was too great to imagine, almost too great to experience.

He knew that it was perfect, that he had found her at last and that he could never let her go. He knew that he would never be unhappy again, that no matter how the world felt about them they were together now and forever, that no force on earth could part them.

She knew that she had found her man and that she would never leave him or let him leave her, that the world was a good place now and that it would be a good place as long as they were together. She cried with joy.

And it got better for them, and better and better. And the sky went dark and then blazed suddenly for a shadow of time with a bright blue flame.

Higher.

Higher...

And then, with a deafening roar, it happened. At once, for both of them, it happened.

The world was bright with joy.

"The others," he said, much later. "Were there many of them, darling?"

"Would it make any difference?"

"None at all," he said honestly. "I just wondered. You don't have to tell me."

"There were two."

He nodded.

"And they weren't that good... for me. You're the only man who has ever been good for me, darling. The only one that ever will be."

He said: "I love you."

"And I love you."

She was lying with her head on his arm. Her face was buried in his chest and she was inhaling the fragrance of him. He was wonderful.

"I didn't think it could be that good," he told her. "Isn't that funny? That's the line the little virgin is supposed to hand the experienced lover. I've got it backwards. But it's true. You are like possessing a woman for the first time."

With a wisdom beyond her years she said: "Maybe I'm the first woman you ever possessed."

"Maybe."

He stroked her hair, her forehead. He kissed her eyes and her nose.

She yawned like a tired little girl.

Sleepily he reached for his shirt, found a pack of cigarettes in the pocket. He found matches as well and lit two cigarettes, one for himself and one for her. They smoked in silence. From time to time he would reach out a hand to stroke her and she would purr like a kitten.

"Forever," he said.

She nodded.

"We'll get married," he said. "I don't know how. It'll be tough. Your folks will raise hell."

"We'll manage."

"Nancy'll give me a divorce." he said. "I'm pretty sure she will. And then we can be married. I don't know if you're old enough to get married in this state or not. Not without parental consent, and they won't give it."

"Then we'll live in sin," she said.

"It won't be sin."

"Not for us."

"And we will get married," he said. "If you're nutty enough to marry an old man."

"You're not so old."

"Pretty old."

"I'm pretty young," she said. "Won't you mind being married to a schoolgirl?"

"Not if she's you."

She kissed him. She put out her cigarette on the linoleum, and she kissed his face and his neck. And then she remembered what she had done with Jeff Gardner, and how horrible it had been for her. And she thought about it now, with Dave, and she knew that the same thing which had been so revolting to her then would not be revolting at all with Dave. It would be good with him, good and clean and sweet.

There was a difference. There was a difference between love with a stranger and love with someone you loved.

A big difference.

All the difference in the world.

Slowly she began to cover him with kisses. She felt him responding to her and she felt very deeply in love with him, very glad of what she was doing.

"You don't have to," he said aloud. "That's not something you have to do, darling."

"But I want to," she said.

"Are you sure?"

"Very sure, my darling."

Her head swam with happiness. Love was wonderful. Love could make all the difference in the world.

•　　　•　　　•

"Dave?"

He opened his eyes. She was on the bed beside him. She was dressed now.

"You looked so happy asleep that I didn't have the heart to wake you. But we'd better get home now. It's getting pretty late."

"What time is it?"

"Your watch says a quarter to twelve."

He nodded thoughtfully and slipped out of bed, finding his clothes and putting them on. "Is it all right?" he asked. "Bringing you home at this hour, I mean."

"I never get home much earlier when I baby-sit."

"You picked a real baby this time."

She laughed. He finished getting dressed and they left the motel and walked to his car. He drove and she sat with her head on his shoulder, a dreamy expression on her face. She was happy. So was he.

He drove, found her house. He stopped in front of it and pulled her to him and they kissed.

"I'll call you tomorrow," he said.

"Okay."

"We'll work something out. Don't worry about it. We'll be married and we'll live happily ever after."

She kissed him again, quickly, and hurried from the car. He watched her until she opened the door and stepped inside. Then he drove around the corner and parked his car in his own driveway. He got out and walked to the front door, then let himself in with his own key.

He looked around for Nancy, found out that she was not home. He wondered if she suspected anything and decided that it didn't matter. He would tell her as soon as she got home. There was no point in keeping it from her any longer. He wouldn't give her all the details, wouldn't mention Lucy by name.

But he would let her know how things stood. He knew that what he felt for Nancy was not love and had not been love for years. In fact he was sure that he had never felt anything for Nancy approaching what he felt now for Lucy.

So he would tell her. And, because she was a decent person, everything would work itself out. He felt sure of that.

He wondered how things would go for him and Lucy. It would be a rough road—that much was obvious. But between the two of them they could make it work. They loved each other—and he was just beginning to realize what a powerful force love was. Everything would work out. He was sure it would. With both of them working together, pulling with all their combined strength, no force on earth could keep them apart.

He lit a cigarette, shook out the match, exhaled clouds of smoke. He checked his watch—it was a few minutes after twelve. Nancy would be home shortly, by all odds.

He smoked. He sat down in the chair in front of the television set but did not turn the set on. He waited for Nancy to come home and rehearsed what he would tell her in his mind.

CHAPTER 10

The funny part of it was that Nancy and Bobby had left the house just ten minutes before Dave arrived. After a spirited bout of love-making the two of them had managed to work up a gigantic appetite between them. Nancy had wanted to whip up something in the kitchen, but the idea of hamburgers at a drive-in had been more appealing to Bobby. So, while Dave was waiting for Nancy, they were devouring hamburgers.

Then, when Bobby dropped Nancy back at her house, the tall blonde saw the car in the garage. Dave was home. It was time to get the show on the road.

"If you want," Bobby said, "I'll come in with you. It might be easier to tell him with someone along for moral support. Just say the word."

Nancy shook her head.

"I wouldn't get in the way," Bobby assured her. "I'd just be there in the background in case he tried something. I've got a mean right, you know."

"He wouldn't do anything."

"You sure?"

"He's a . . . nice guy," Nancy said. "He's not what I want but he's still a nice guy."

"Men are men, you know."

"I know. But I can manage alone. And you don't have to worry about me, Bobby. I made a promise and I'll stick to it. I couldn't back out now if I wanted to. And believe me, I don't want to. I'm getting the divorce no matter what happens."

A kiss.

Then Nancy left the car and watched Bobby drive away into the night. She walked to the front door with her words ringing in her ears.

The words were true. Before, Nancy had to admit to herself, she had not been so certain about the divorce. Even with Bobby on the phone she had been a bit doubtful. She had insisted that the divorce was certain, but her words were surer than her mind. Now, however, her mind was made up. She would ask Dave at once. She would tell him as much as she had to. And, eventually, everything would work itself out.

She walked to the door, pausing when she saw him in the living room. He was seated in front of the television set but the set did not seem to be on. He looked as though he was waiting for someone. She wondered what if anything he suspected. Well, it didn't matter. He would learn everything there was to know in a matter of minutes. He would find out the truth about her and he would accept the inevitable.

And that would be that.

She fished in her purse for her key, found it, and fitted it in the door. She turned, then shoved the door open and walked into the house. She closed the door after her, then continued on into the living room.

"I have to talk to you," he said.

"I know," she said. "I know. I've been meaning to . . . just a minute, Dave."

She left him there while she took off her jacket and hung it on a hanger in the closet. Then she returned to him and sat down on the sofa.

She opened her mouth to speak. But before she could get a word out he had begun and she could not interrupt. She had to hear him out.

And when she heard what he was saying her mouth dropped open and she couldn't believe her ears.

He said: "I . . . I want a divorce, Nancy."

It was a very weird scene.

He was sitting in a chair and she was sitting on the sofa. First, in level tones, he explained his situation. He had found another woman. He was in love with this other woman. He wanted Nancy to divorce him so that he and this other woman could get married.

He spoke haltingly but he did not stop once he got started. He told her everything but the name of the girl. He told her that it was not her fault, that she had been a fine wife to him, that he felt like an utter cad, but that there was no way to help the situation that had developed.

She heard him out. She listened to everything he had to say, and then, when he finally seemed to have run out of words, it was her turn.

She realized with a start that she did not have to say a word. She could give in grudgingly, agree to divorce him, and never mention how she herself felt about the whole thing. That way, she knew, she could rook him for a huge property settlement and a healthy cut of alimony.

But it was not fair to do this. Nor was it fair to agree to the divorce without making her own position known to him. He was her husband. He had a right to know.

So she told him.

She did not take the easy way out by saying that it was another man in whom she was interested. She put her cards right on the table face up.

"I'm in love, too," she said, almost enjoying the jolt of surprise that overwhelmed him at once. So she jolted him once more.

"I'm in love with a woman, Dave. That's right. I'm not kidding, Dave. I'm a lesbian. It sounds funny to hear myself saying it but it's the truth. I'm a lesbian."

Then she began to talk about Bobby, about the way they had met and the way they had fallen in love. She reminisced about Sondra and their love affair, and she told him of the overwhelming frustration of their marriage.

"I don't want you to think it was your fault," she was careful to emphasize. "You were a man. That was the essence of the ... problem ... right there. I couldn't have loved any man. Believe me, I didn't realize that when I married you. I've never had anything to do with any other man. Until I met this girl ... I was a perfect wife. I mean, I didn't have any affairs or anything. Not until this one."

He had a hard time believing that she was a lesbian. In his eyes lesbians and homosexuals were people who lived on other planets. They didn't really exist. It was unthinkable that his own wife could be like that.

But eventually it sank in. She was telling the truth and he had to accept it.

So, because of what she had told him, because she had held nothing back, he told her the full story. How it was impossible for him to love a mature woman. How he had developed a paralyzing yen for young girls, how he had gone to child prostitutes in order to satisfy his strange hungers.

And now, finally, he had met a sixteen-year-old girl and had genuinely fallen in love with her.

They talked on into the night. They found out things about each other that they had never known, had never suspected. They held nothing back.

At the end they agreed on a divorce. He would give her a final cash settlement which both agreed was fair. Then they would part, with no hard feelings and no misgivings.

Then at last they were finished. She went up to bed; he stretched out alone on the couch. They both felt unbelievably fresh and clean and free.

The divorce was easily accomplished. The next day Dave found a Mexican lawyer residing in New York who made a good living arranging quick and painless divorces. They saw him together and Dave signed the necessary papers. Then Nancy and Bobby boarded a plane for Mexico City.

In Mexico City the divorce was granted in a matter of minutes. Nancy and Bobby found a plush room at a plush hotel on the Reforma. They went to bull fights and drank tequila and made wild love.

They returned from Mexico finally. Bobby sold the small shop in Mataquois, knowing that it would be impossible to get along in that environment.

"People are too snoopy," she explained to Nancy. "We want a nice place where nobody gives a damn how we live. Manhattan. That's the place."

Manhattan was the place. To be precise, Greenwich Village was the place. As Bobby explained to Nancy, if you want to hide a tree, you put it in a forest. If you want to hide lesbianism, you move it to Greenwich Village.

The Village was a new life for Nancy. She met other girls like herself, other lesbians, ranging from girls who looked like men to girls far more feminine than herself. She found bars where gay girls hung out all day and all night. She went to parties, parties where women who loved women sat around in a circle drinking chianti straight from the bottle. She met people the same as herself, people from whom she had nothing to hide.

And she was happy.

It was Bobby who found the apartment. The apartment was located on Barrow Street, one of the quiet streets in the West Village. They rented the apartment unfurnished and moved Bobby's furniture into it.

Soon the apartment sang with Bartok string quartets. And the bed in the bedroom—a huge double bed built for comfort—vibrated with the strains of love.

Their lovemaking was superb. Nancy never tired of taking her pleasures with Bobby's magnificent body. She would wake up in the morning, her fingers ready to caress, to stroke, to pet. She would wake Bobby with a kiss every day, and every day she found a different part of Bobby to kiss.

Then a Bartok quartet would be spinning atonally on the hi-fi. And then Bobby's body would be nestled with Nancy's body, and Bobby would be pressing against Nancy.

It was heavenly.

Magnificent.

And Nancy knew that as long as they were together they would be happy.

Very happy.

And, she knew also that, they would be together forever.

It was a little different for Dave and Lucy.

To begin with, they faced a different problem. Lucy was sixteen. She had a pair of parents who would not look too kindly upon her marrying a man eighteen years older than herself. She had a position in high school. She was a minor in the eyes of society.

This made things difficult.

But not impossible.

Nothing was impossible.

Not for them.

Lucy's parents were the first obstacle. And Lucy's parents were not going to be moved by appeals to reason. So Dave and Lucy did not attempt to be rational. They simply confronted the Kings with a force which could not be resisted.

"We're going to be married," Dave said. "With or without

your blessing, we are going to be married. You can try to stop us but it won't work. We're in love. And we're getting married. That's all there is to it."

That was not all there was to it, Mr. King pointed out. Lucy was a minor. They could get a court order forbidding Dave to see her. They could have him thrown in jail. They could do any one of a number of things.

"But," Dave said, "you won't."

The Kings stared.

"You won't," Dave said, "because you love your daughter. You don't want to ruin her life. You don't want her to hate you forever, do you?"

They didn't.

And, although it was a little more complex than that, that more or less turned the trick. The Kings gave in because they had very little choice in the matter. Dave and Lucy were married with the consent—unwillingly given, but given nevertheless—of Lucy's parents.

Married.

Other problems remained. First of all there was his job. It did not come as a tremendous shock to Dave that his employers no longer wished to have him in their employ. He had more or less anticipated that.

"So we go elsewhere," he told Lucy. "We can't live here any more. Not in this town, not near these people. It's no good for us, darling. We've got to find a new place."

"It doesn't matter where we go," she said. "Just so we go there together."

"You sure?"

"Positive," she said.

"You happy?"

"The happiest."

"Content?"

"Very."

He caressed her thigh. "Anything I can do to make you a little bit happier?"

She purred.

"Anything at all?"

She moaned. And she grabbed him and drew him down and told him just what he could do.

He followed her instructions.

Letter for letter.

The town where they wound up was Dallas. New York was a bust as far as Dave was concerned. He was sick of it anyway, sick of the pace, the pressure, the ridiculous drive you had to have to make it in the advertising business. It was fine if you were single, fine if you were married but your marriage didn't matter to you.

But he was married now, in a marriage that did matter to him. He didn't need to blow off steam in a Manhattan advertising agency. He had a woman to take care of him in that respect, and Lucy was much better than writing commercials for the Krutchmeir-Philbert people.

He sold the house and they flew to Dallas. They stayed at a hotel while he sent out feelers to a half-dozen local agencies. One of them called him for an interview.

He went to the interview armed to the teeth. The attaché case he carried was crammed to capacity with samples of his work.

He tossed his stuff on the desk and let the grey-haired man pore over it.

"Good," the man said. "Very good. Can I see your references now?"

Dave laughed. "My character references wouldn't do me much good," he said. "Maybe I don't have much character. I left my wife and married a sixteen-year-old girl."

"Worse things have happened," the agency man said.

"So I'm not much of a character," Dave went on. "I can tell you all the bad things about me that you could possibly want to know. You don't need to call my references."

"To hell with the bad things," the agency man said. "I want to hear good things. Tell me some good things, Grantland. Good things about you."

Dave grinned. "I can write the best damned copy you ever saw," he said.

The agency man's grin matched his own. "That's good talk," he said. "Right good talk. The kind I wanted to hear in the first place. I think I'm going to hire you, Grantland. I think you're going to fit in just fine."

Which was precisely what happened.

They found a house for sale and they grabbed it. Lucy went out and selected furniture, discovering in the process that furnishing a house was a hell of a lot more exciting than doing term papers for history class. Dave encouraged her and she got interested in the subject. While he worked at the agency she went to the Dallas Public Library and studied interior decoration. She got pretty deeply interested in it.

And wound up in business. She didn't get rich helping women

make their homes look good, any more than Dave got rich helping local stores sell their merchandise. But she was happy, and he was happy, and all was well.

Which brings us to the end. Two girls live in Greenwich Village. A man and a girl live in Dallas. Before, a man and a woman lived "naturally" in Long Island and both were miserable.

That which is natural is not always good. That which is good is not always natural.

Nancy and Bobby know this. Dave and Lucy know this. And their twisted lives are better for the knowledge.

My Newsletter: I get out an email newsletter at unpredictable intervals, but rarely more often than every other week. I'll be happy to add you to the distribution list. A blank email to lawbloc@gmail.com with "newsletter" in the subject line will get you on the list, and a click of the "Unsubscribe" link will get you off it, should you ultimately decide you're happier without it.

Lawrence Block has been writing award-winning mystery and suspense fiction for half a century. You can read his thoughts about crime fiction and crime writers in *The Crime of Our Lives*, where this MWA Grand Master tells it straight. His most recent novels are *The Girl With the Deep Blue Eyes*; *The Burglar Who Counted the Spoons*, featuring Bernie Rhodenbarr; *Hit Me,* featuring Keller; and *A Drop of the Hard Stuff,* featuring Matthew Scudder, played by Liam Neeson in the film *A Walk Among the Tombstones.* Several of his other books have been filmed, although not terribly well. He's well known for his books for writers, including the classic *Telling Lies for Fun & Profit,* and *The Liar's Bible.* In addition to prose works, he has written episodic television (*Tilt!*) and the Wong Kar-wai film, *My Blueberry Nights.* He is a modest and humble fellow, although you would never guess as much from this biographical note.

Email: lawbloc@gmail.com
Twitter: @LawrenceBlock
Facebook: lawrence.block
Website: lawrenceblock.com

www.ingramcontent.com/pod-product-compliance
Lightning Source LLC
Chambersburg PA
CBHW060942180626
46817CB00004B/1680